Winsley Walker
and
Other Flying Objects

To: Nana
& Sophie,

May you always
soar high above the
crowd !

Winsley Walker
and
Other Flying Objects

♡, Nancy

by
Nancy Cadle Craddock

11/2014

First Edition: August 2014

ISBN: 978-1500750527

For my granddaughter Kaitlyn
who loves a good book

~ Contents ~

~~~~~~ AFTER Hinkle's Hissie Fit ~~~~~~

Chapter 1

~ HINKLE'S HISSIE FIT ~

When my brother's teacher burst through the double doors over at the elementary school, I didn't think it had anything to do with me, or any of us Walkers for that matter.

After all, it was a Tuesday, and not even noon yet. The trouble-makers in my family didn't usually stir up trouble until late in the afternoon. Unless of course, it was the weekend.

I was the good one, unlike my eight-year-old brother Billy. Mama often said it was on account of the way I was *raised*. Gramps would always fire back that once in a while some Walker was just *born* different from the rest. Either way, I made sure my name was never mixed-up in anything that could get me screamed at, in the paper, or worse . . . dead.

You could feel all of that changing before the elementary doors slammed shut, sending my name through the air crumbled up among the stomping and loud mutterings of one crazy old witch.

"Winsley Walker! Don't you *dare* move until I've had a word with you!"

I wanted to look away but couldn't ignore all the high-pitched commotion, and from the startled expressions on nearby faces, neither could anyone else. Among the swirling dust and scattered words, there she was: Old Bat Hinkle, the meanest teacher to ever prowl the linoleum halls of Cross Lanes Elementary. Her eyes were fireballs and her arms pumped like the wings of a goose being chased by a dog. As Hinkle sprinted onto the middle school grounds toward me, I prayed to hear the piercing sound of the Fire Drill bell.

Silence. *Of course.*

Stopping only inches from the stone wall where I sat with other brown baggers, spit and words sprayed from Hinkle's pasty white lips. "Reckon you know why I'm here."

Wedged between Dimples Cheeksly and the new kid, I tried to answer, but my "no, ma'am" got twisted up with the peanut butter and jelly working its way down my throat.

I reached for my open thermos of milk.

Before I had time to wash everything down,

Hinkle ranted on. "What's all this nonsense about that crackpot grandfather of yours? Heard he's aiming to build himself an air-o-plane. P-l-e-e-e-a-s-e tell me he's *not* doing something so utterly ri-dic-u-lous!"

"Yes, ma'am ... I mean ... no, ma'am." I tried to shake a "no", but couldn't get my bobbing head to match my words.

"So it's true? That same idiot who thought he could turn a truckload of Mexican Jumping Beans into some crazy anti-gravity device wants to become a PILOT! I doubt he could find his way over to the capitol in Charleston, much less through the clouds in something homemade. Well, I've got news for you Walkers. EVERYONE in CROSS LANES ... no ... EVERYONE in the entire state of WEST VIRGINIA is laughing their heads off."

More spit. *Great, just great!*

Hinkle continued, "Listen here, girlie ... and make no mistake about it, if by chance he does get some contraption to fly, he'd better not come crashing down on any of us. Understand?"

"Yes," I squeaked, fighting the urge to throw the last of my milk at her.

As if reading my mind, Hinkle gave me the old "stink-eye" and turned away.

With jerky movements, she thumped across weedy grass, leaving several "tsks" in the air behind her.

Right up until the last "tsk" escaped her clenched

teeth and pinched mouth, I'd done all in my power to sabotage Gramps's plans to build airplane. Now, Hinkle's spitty words changed everything.

Although he didn't know it yet, Gramps had a new partner. From now on, things would be different. We'd show that old hag, and all of Cross Lanes, too! Gramps's heap of rusted metal, busted-out windshields and old wheel-barrow tires would fly if I had to build the dang thing and heave it in the air – all by myself.

As Hinkle disappeared through the doors of the middle school, I let out a sigh of relief along with every other sixth grader within earshot. Then, except for some squawking bird in a tree somewhere, everything and everyone went silent.

I drank the last of my milk, threw the thermos in my lunchbox, and snapped the tin box shut, all without so much as a glance at Barbie on the front. I kept my eyes on my scuffed-up Oxfords and hugged my lunchbox to my chest as the sound of snickering made its way toward me.

Dimples scooted closer and slung her arm around my shoulder. "Want my puddin'?"

I looked up. Everyone but Dimples melted away. She handed me her spoon and a small Tupperware cup of chocolate pudding.

I'm not sure if it was the pudding or Dimples's arm around my shoulder, but all of a sudden I wanted to chase Hinkle down and give her a piece of my mind. After all, it was a free country, and if my wacky grandfather wanted to build himself an airplane, then by golly, why shouldn't he?

As cafeteria kids made their way outside, I tucked a strand of my brown hair behind my ear and gave the spoon and Tupperware back to Dimples.

Soon, we'd be choosing teams for kickball as if nothing had happened. Of course, in small towns like Cross Lanes, things are rarely what they seem. This wouldn't be the first time something involving us Walkers would be repeated from one end of the Kanawha Valley to the other before the sun went down. But for now, Dimples and I followed the crowd to a grassy field. As we walked, Dimples whispered, "Don't let Hinkle's hissie-fit get to you. She hates *everyone*."

I nodded. "I thought we'd seen the last of that old witch when we left elementary."

"Aw . . . she's a looney bird," Dimples replied.

"Can you believe she left a room full of second graders, including my own brother, to blast me? No wonder her students act like chimpanzees."

Dimples replied, "Well now, we don't really know *why* she came. You'd hope it wasn't just to cause a ruckus, but who knows? Anyway, Shirley Undertaker told my mother that Hinkle's been hittin' the bottle a lot lately and she's plannin' to retire."

"Really?"

Dimples took a gulp of air and glanced sideways at me. "Yep . . . and my mom said she didn't know how Hinkle lasted this long . . . and that your brother was enough to drive even the fiercest of teachers out the classroom and down to Myrtle . . . or end the school year with a drinking habit they hadn't had before the name *Billy Walker* showed up on their class roll."

"Myrtle . . . Myrtle Beach?"

"That's where all teachers go when they retire. Didn't you know that?" Dimples answered with a raised eyebrow.

I shook my head. "But why should Billy be the one blamed if that old bat ends up drunk on the beach? Besides, look at me . . . I've been around that jerky kid my whole life and you don't see me drinking or moving to Myrtle."

Dimples gave me a pity smile.

I answered Dimple's pity smile by sticking out my tongue.

Dimples and her mom, Mrs. Cheeksly, were probably right, but I couldn't help feeling somewhat defensive about Billy. After all, that little booger *was* my brother.

Dimples dropped her lunchbox on top of others already on the ground. "Winsley, I didn't want to be the one to tell you, but the whole town is getting more and more riled-up about your Gramps and this airplane-thing. I can't go anywhere without hearing something about it."

Feeling even more defensive, I straightened my

shoulders and lifted my chin, "Ah, I'm sure he knows what he's doing."

As I took my place in line, I thought about Hinkle, Gramps, and how a couple spoonfuls of pudding had promoted Dimples from being just another annoying classmate to a share-your-dessert kind of friend, and by the time my turn came to kick an old lopsided red ball, I was determined to build an airplane – or die trying. I mean, how hard could it be, for cryin'-out-loud?

Chapter 2

~ THE TREEHOUSE INCIDENT ~

(THE EVEnts leading up to Hinkle's Hissie Fit)

The month leading up to Hinkle's little hissie-fit seemed normal. Well . . . at least . . . for us Walkers.

My younger brother Billy and I lived next door to our grandparents. This may sound like fun to some kids. It probably would be too, if you had sweet, doting grandparents who bought you toys and gave you candy. Our grandparents believed old toys were as good as new, and we should be thankful we had a full set of teeth, cavity-free.

Toys and teeth aside, I had other things to worry about, odds-and-ends stuff I *didn't* want to happen. Unfortunately, all of it involved the two least likely to change their ways: Gramps and Billy. Worse, everyone else in my family seemed too busy to give a hoot about what those two were up to, except me . . . and Mama, on occasion.

I went looking for Granny to talk about my worries and found her in the kitchen punching down dough.

"Granny, when you were my age, did you worry about things?"

"I guess I did my fair share of frettin'," Granny answered, throwing a punch so hard her fist landed with a loud smack against the bottom of the bowl.

I coaxed a finger full of gooey dough from the rim of the bowl.

Granny swatted at my hand. "That dough's raw, young lady . . . besides, what's you got to be fearful about?"

I popped the dough into my mouth. "Ev-we-wing."

Granny stopped punching and handed me a glass of water. "Here, drink up so you can talk straight."

After a loud gulp, I answered, "Everything."

"Well now, that sure sounds like a mighty big heap of worry."

"Sure is," I answered, taking another swig of water.

"Winsley-girl, why don't you write those worries of yours down? Maybe that way, they won't feel so fierce."

I pulled another finger-full of dough from the bowl. "It'd take forever to write 'em all."

Granny gave the dough another hard punch. "Just try gettin' the big ones down. You can work your way to the little ones later."

"But there's so many of 'em."

"Write 'em . . . fight 'em . . . or try to forget 'em. It's up to you," Granny replied.

"Guess I'll write 'em, then."

I licked dough from my fingertips before fishing around in Granny's junk drawer for something that would write. After sorting through ancient receipts, old church bulletins and recipes, my fingers landed on a ballpoint pen advertising Rod's Car Lot and a half-used spiral notebook. I pulled both of them out and stuffed the rest back in the drawer. After making sure the ballpoint worked and ripping out doodled-on pages from the spiral, I slung myself down in a chair at Granny's kitchen table.

The front of the spiral was missing so the first page would have to do for the cover, and since I didn't know exactly how many pages I'd need, I decided to use it for the first of my worries, too, as I picked up the ballpoint pen to write:

THis NotEbook BElongs to

WinslEY WalkER

~ Worry #1 ~

We're going to get kicked out of West Virginia on account of Billy or Gramps - or both!

Cradling the bowl of dough in her arms, Granny walked my way. Standing beside me, she bent down and hummed a strange new tune as I continued.

~ Worry #2 ~

A trip to the Looney Bin is in Mother's Future when she cracks (and she will) from living next door to her in-laws.

Still clutching the bowl of dough, Granny bent closer to my ear. The humming grew louder and her little tune took on an angry beat as she gave the dough a right hook that would be the envy of any prize-winning fighter.

I flinched and added :

GRanny doesn't count,

It's GRaMPS I'M talking about.

As I stared at my worries, Granny's humming softened but I began to sweat.

Unfortunately, on paper, my worries looked as fierce as ever.

Daddy once said *ninety-eight* percent of the things you worry about never come to pass. When I asked about the other *two* percent, he just shrugged. Not knowing what to think, I clung to the hope that my worries fell in the *ninety-eight percent* Bucket-of-Life and everything would turn out okay in the end.

But on the day Gramps stated, "Gonna build you kids a treehouse, one that's at least six feet off the ground," Billy and I should have been sportin' t-shirts with "*Two Percenters*" printed smack across our chest.

A couple of weeks later, and against my better judgment, Billy and I scrambled up a rope ladder dangling from our new treehouse for the very first time.

Down on the ground, Gramps exclaimed, "This

here's one for the record books. Hey, *Building Woodworkers* buys ideas for their magazine. I'm gonna draw up my tree house plans and send 'em in." With that, Gramps slid a pencil out from the top of his ear and said, "The way I figure it, if you kids can have some fun and I can make a little money at the same time, all the better."

From our perch in the sky, we watched as Gramps took a small notepad from his back pocket and began to sketch.

We laughed as we spotted Granny pouring bird-seed in a feeder, the mailman coming up the drive-way and Billy's friend Leo Undertaker shooting hoops in his driveway at the bottom of the hill.

Then, out of nowhere, the wind kicked up.

As the tree swayed, I reached for Billy's hand and pulled him down on the floor by me.

Immediately, he jerked his hand away and stood back up. "Let go of me."

I tried to grab his hand again to pull him back down but he escaped my grasp. "Billy, get down!"

"You're not my boss!" he yelled as he used his hands and feet to rock the tree house harder from side-to-side – on purpose!

"Stop rocking us!" I yelled up at him.

Billy continued. "I'll do what I wanna do."

"Stop it, Billy," I yelled louder over the woosh of the wind.

His only answer was "Hey, everybody, watch this".

I closed my eyes and trembled as the boards beneath my feet grew more violent with each gust of wind and Billy's wild rocking.

As the hair on the back of my head covered my face, I heard a loud pop.

And then, the floor tilted.

Through straggly strands of hair, I watched Billy tumble, his head hitting mine, forcing my head to hit the floor as a loud pop signaled disaster.

I grabbed Billy's waist with one hand and the rope ladder with my other as we were pitched downward.

Boards rained down around us, bouncing this-way-and-that.

After everything happened, the wind died, leaving Billy and me sprawled on the ground. Two popped-out cords of Mother's clothesline weaved in-and-out around us like an albino garden snake.

With a damp washcloth on top of my head, I scrambled to the top of the pile of half-dry clothes, clothespins and boards, pulling Billy with me. His arms flapped through the openings of a pair of dad's boxer shorts. We surveyed the damage and what little was left of the tree house as it rested against the last three cords of Mother's clothesline. Worse, when everything came to a stop, Mama's best brassiere, her red one, was flying at the top of an old elm tree. There we stood, our mouths open, as we watched it flap wildly in front of the whole wide world.

Someone must have phoned the fire department, fearing some of us half-dead or dying. And in no time at all, I'd be hard-pressed to say who or what wailed the loudest that day, the red fire engine as it roared up the hill or Mother as she shrieked in embarrassment.

Neighbors stood snickering in the driveway.

I heard Shirley Undertaker say, "You'd think even the kids would know better than to go up in anything Old Man Walker put together, wouldn't ya?"

Elsie Dunlap answered, "I declare, nothin' any of this bunch does comes as any surprise. Still . . . just when you think you've seen it all."

I wanted to shout at all of the neighbors to go away, watching what I never thought I'd see, a fireman walking toward Mother with the strap of her red brassiere pinched between his fingertips.

Without a doubt, things were literally crashing down around us, faster than anyone could spit.

Worse, now we were drawing a crowd. *Great. Just great.*

And Gramps . . . the last I'd seen of him was when he saluted Mother's bra as if it was Old Glory, before he turned and sauntered away.

As I pulled leaves from my hair and swiped a damp sock from my shoulder, I spotted Gramps's treehouse plans poking out from the leg of what were my freshly-washed-and-hanging-on-the-line-to-dry "Tuesday" panties. As I reached for Tuesday, I was able to grab Friday, too. Shoving both into my pocket, I wondered what *Building Woodworkers* would have to say about all of this.

Chapter 3

~ A REALLY BAD IDEA ~

Even though summer was working its way toward our little valley, we were still a month away from freedom.

It seemed like I was marking days off the calendar until school was out faster than Hinkle could spit. But until I could make that last red check, I prayed for the floor to swallow me every time that old witch burst through the door of my fifth grade classroom, screaming, "Winsley, see that your parents get this note! Honestly, I don't know how much more of Billy Ray Walker I can take!"

Whenever she flung some folded up piece of paper my way, it was all I could do not to shout back, "Well, neither do I!"

Why should it be MY fault whenever Billy slapped or elbowed his way to the water fountain, or conked some second grader over the head? According to Billy, the one usually carrying on was Hinkle herself, not some stunned kid with a red handprint up the side of their face.

Even so, I'd only drop every third or fourth note on the kitchen counter at the end of the day. The rest I buried in Billy's sock drawer. It seemed like a good way to encourage him to behave every time he put his socks and shoes on for school.

Often, Hinkle's notes ended up as teeny little spit wads lodged on the back of some poor soul's head come Sunday morning at church. The longer the sermon, the more the spit wads flew.

Even I had to admit "Spit-wad Sundays" were a lot more fun than watching Mother's contorted face whenever she got sight of one of Hinkle's notes. So, yes, I hide a lot of notes. I was for anything that didn't end up swirling around in the dreaded *Hinkle Note Cycle*:

~ THE HINKLE NOTE CYCLE ~

1. Billy torments some poor little tyke.
2. Hinkle scribbles it all down in a note.
3. Hinkle gives the note to me.
4. I tote the note home and either
   a. stuff it in Billy's socks (Nothing Happens)

    b. giVE it to MotHER (FiRE Rains Down).
5. MotHER YElls at DaddY about BillY.
6. DaddY PunisHES BillY.
7. BillY gEts EVEn witH mE!

So, when it was all said and done, I might as well have smacked the side of my own head.

Worse, I was still weeks away from making that end-of-the-year check on the calendar when the mailman robbed me of settling into the doing nothingness of summer.

Yes, all hope of happiness came crashing down one Saturday when Granny sent me to the mailbox and a "You Can Build Anything" catalog poked its head out alongside the electric bill.

Before I had time to run and hide it, Granny yelled through the screen door, "Quit dawdling, girl, and bring the mail on in here."

By the time I reluctantly handed the catalog over to Granny, I was already feeling the heebie-jeebies from skimming over page one: *Creating Nuclear Fusion in the Kitchen Sink.*

Holding onto the back of one of Granny's ladder-back chairs to steady my trembling legs, I asked, "Who comes up with this stuff . . . and who in the heck would shell out good money to buy it?"

"People hoping to make a quick buck . . . foolish people . . . dreamers . . . that's who." After flipping to "Raising Alligators for Fun and Profit at Home in Your Bathtub", Granny reached for an old syrup bottle of her homemade "White Lightning" and took a long sip.

I bit my nails, knowing we had "hoping to make a quick buck, foolish and a dreamer" all rolled into one body: Gramps.

And sure enough, it didn't take him long to find it buried beneath coffee grounds in the trash. After brushing away the coffee grounds, he opened the catalog and thumbed back-and-forth, reading every page.

The longer he looked, the faster butterflies fluttered in my stomach. To make matters worse, I suddenly developed an every-now-and-again twitch in my right eye.

I tried to set my worries aside but I couldn't shake a nagging feeling some of us were bound to get hurt, or maybe even die from some awful experiment gone awry. As Gramps made his way to his side of the house – the garage – I begged Granny to put a stop to all of the nonsense. But it was late in the day, and she was doing what she always did when she had one-nip-too-many. She was singing "She'll be Coming Round the Mountain" over-and-over at the top of her lungs.

I entered the garage and took my usual seat. I swung my legs and twirled this way-and-that atop an old stool as I watched him thumb back and forth through that wretched little catalog.

Hoping to distract him, I said, "That stuff looks expensive."

Gramps didn't answer.

I tried again. "Much too expensive for the likes of us, don'tcha think?"

"Maybe so. Maybe so. But . . . it'd be worth it," Gramps answered, standing beside me. He continued to flip through the pages. "Yes . . . sir . . . it'd be worth it."

Before I could think of a good reply, Gramps licked his thumb and used it to work two stuck pages apart.

With my stomach butterflies in a flying frenzy, I stopped twirling and leaned closer.

Gramps let out a low whistle as the pages separated. "Well, won't you looky here. Something's been hiding."

My eyes followed his index finger and then, nearly popped out of my head when they landed on a sketch of an extremely small plane with three round windows. Above it were the words *Emerald Eyes*. On the opposite page sat a shorter, squattier model under the words *Sailing Skies*.

"I've got a mind to order plans for one of these," Gramps muttered.

"You'd better talk to Granny about this," I replied, with a twitch. My stomach butterflies now looped slowly from side to side as if they, too, were drunk on White Lightning. I glanced to make sure Gramps's trash can was in its usual place, in case I needed to throw up.

"Nah, she won't care. Anyway, I'm my own boss.

What do you think, Winnie-girl, which one should I get?" Gramps asked, without looking up.

I picked up a hammer and gave the corner of Gramps's workbench a hard whack. "I think she *will* care and you'd better ask for her permission."

He didn't seem to be listening, so I whacked the hammer again and studied both pictures carefully. Finally, I pointed to *Sailing Skies* simply because there weren't any windows and it looked the least likely to hold passengers.

Gramps continued to examine both pages. "Well . . . now . . . we need to consider everything, don't you think?"

Without waiting for me to answer, Gramps talked on. "A shorter plane would be faster to build . . . and it seems to me, she might be faster in the air. Less parts to buy . . . but . . . considering my plans for her, I think we may have a "winner" here with old *Emerald Eyes*."

Now, my head hurt along with my queasy stomach.

Then, like a bolt from the sky, I had the solution! And in that second-or-two, I almost felt sorry for Gramps. *Almost*. But mainly, I felt happy that we Walkers would stay alive! There'd be no homemade plane. Poor, poor Gramps. He wouldn't get his way after all.

I cleared my throat. "Gramps, I think you're forgetting one little thing."

"What's that, girl?"

"You don't have a pilot's license so building a plane would be a waste of your time."

"Well, now, girlie-girl, I don't remember reading anything about the Wright Brothers needing a license, do you? So, why should I?"

"But ... but ... Gramps ... that was a long time ago."

Gramps didn't look up from the catalog. "The law's the law. And we're all created equal under it. Isn't that right?"

"I guess so."

"Well, then, I don't need no license either."

His logic, as usual, didn't quite hit the mark, but how can you argue with something like that. So, I gave my stool a twirl and thought some more. Maybe if I couldn't get the catalog away from Gramps, I could get Gramps's mind away from the catalog.

"Are you sure, Gramps? Are you really sure you want to spend your hard-earned money like this? Just think, we could pack up the car and head down to Myrtle Beach for less than the cost for either of those airplanes."

He didn't seem to hear me, much less answer.

More butterflies.

Still holding the hammer, I gave the workbench another whack.

Gramps mumbled something to himself.

I sputtered on. "With all that money, we could probably even go further down the coast, all the way to Florida. Orange juice, alligators, the whole works. Whatdaya think?"

No answer.

Even more butterflies.

Two hammer whacks, a bit harder.

Gramps pulled the catalog closer to his face and said, "Whatda I think? I think we've got a winner here. Yes, siree, she looks like a winner to me. I do believe *Emerald Eyes* might just be the trick."

A million more butterflies.

Three whacks, each one harder than the last.

Gramps looked up and I tried one last time. "Well, I think you're wasting your money. Who knows if you'll get the plans . . . and if you do . . . who knows if that contraption will even fly. The whole thing may be a scam, someone just trying to get your money. Think about it . . . we could all be sitting on the beach, toes in the sand, sippin' juice out of little plastic oranges, all for the price of a bunch of old plans. SEA-AND-SAND *or* old plane plans. C'mon, Gramps . . . say it . . . say SEA-AND-SAND . . . instead of old plane plans."

Being the ornery old thing that he was, he answered. "OLD PLANE PLANS!" causing the hammer in my hand to have a life of its own.

Bang! The hammer barely missed smashing a pencil into little pieces. *Smack!* The hammer dented an old wooden yardstick.

The hammer rose high in the air and made a dive. *Whack!* Without warning, a chip of wood from the corner of Gramps's workbench flew across the garage.

Gramps reached to take back his hammer with one hand and kept his grip on the catalog with the other. "Always did hate gritty old sand in my britches. Now, go on in the house and fetch my checkbook from behind the clock on the mantle. And get me an envelope and a stamp, too."

I wanted to bolt, but I trudged inside for his checkbook and the other stuff.

When I re-entered the garage, Gramps's hammer was nowhere to be seen.

I could barely watch as Gramps made a checkmark by the words *Emerald Eyes* on the order form and wrote out a check. The minute he licked the envelope shut, I gnawed down what was left of the tip of my right thumbnail. And, at that exact moment, the annoying twitch in my right eye became more "now" than "again" while a jillion butterflies settled in for good.

I tried to ease my worries by reminding myself that ordering plans was one thing, buying parts . . . well . . . that was another. That, along with the fact that plane parts were bound to cost a heap, provided me with a glimmer of hope. No matter what he said, I knew Gramps didn't take to spending money lightly.

Later that evening, as the two of us were flying full speed in the porch swing, I cleared my throat and gave it another shot. "Bet parts for *Emerald*

Eyes gonna cost more than hopping aboard one of those nice big roomy commercial jets for a trip to some place nice."

"Can't put a price on the freedom to soar *whenever* you want, Winsley-girl."

"That may be true, Gramps, but if you owned your own plane, wouldn't it be like throwing money away when it's sitting idle on the ground? You know – bad weather and all that."

"In the sky . . . on the ground . . . that little emerald-eyed baby gonna be worth every penny. Yes, siree . . . every penny. And speaking of eyes, what's the matter with yours? You develop a tic or something?"

"Guess so," I answered, trying to stop my twitch, which of course, only made it speed up double-time.

Gramps gave a kick, making my head hit the back of the swing as it lurched. "You oughta go see about it."

"Well, I would if I could, but Dad said we're gonna have to ride less and walk more. Doubt he'd want to use up gasoline on something like a tic. It's not like a tic is an emergency or anything."

"Your dad musta seen that article in the newspaper, the one about the rising price of gasoline," Gramps answered with a swift kick of his foot against the floor of the porch. Another whack of my head. *Dag-nab-it.*

I rubbed the back of my head. "Reckon you may

have to do away with the idea of building an airplane, the cost of gas and all?"

"Are you kiddin'? That plane's gonna make us a ton of money."

A ton of money? My foot skidded across the wooden porch floor. "How do you figure that?" I asked, bringing the swing to a dead stop.

Gramps turned toward me and asked, "Ever heard of the *Waterman Whatsit?*"

"The what?"

"The *Waterman Whatsit,*" he repeated with a hearty laugh and a kick that flung us back again.

"No," I answered above the creak of the swing.

"Some guy by the name of Waldo Waterman built himself a tailless airplane, one that was light and simple to fly. And listen to this . . . that little baby could either zoom through the air or zip down the street – like an automobile! Paraded that thing everywhere."

"Waldo or the plane?" I answered.

"Very funny, girlie-girl . . . you remind me of your grandma when she was young."

I smiled, thinking maybe I'd distracted him.

But being Gramps, he continued, "The plane, of course."

He gave another swift kick. "What's more, from everything I've read, Waldo's itty-bitty plane drew a mighty big crowd. And Winnie-girl, guess what?"

"What?" I asked, not really wanting to know.

"I mean to top the *Whatsit*."

"How?"

"I'm plannin' to build the World's Smallest Passenger Plane! Then, I'm gonna invite the whole world to come and take a look – for a fee, of course."

I prayed the butterflies would escape my stomach and carry me away with them. "Passenger plane! With passengers and everything?"

"You bet."

It was worse than I imagined. Passengers! Other people's lives were now at stake.

Even though I didn't want to encourage him, I had to know how many lives he was planning on endangering. I could barely get the words out "How . . . how . . . how many passengers?"

"Three if they're skinny, two if they're fat. And that doesn't include the pilot – me, of course."

Before Gramps had time to give another kick, I jumped out of the swing. Hands on hips, I replied, "I doubt folks around here would be willing to fork over money to see an airplane – of any kind."

"Oh, they'll pay. Believe you me, they'll be lining up from here-to-there. Plenty of folks. Yes, siree, you can bank on it, Winny-girl. That little plane might very well get us in the record books. Just think of it, we're on the brink of being famous . . . and rich! No more worries, ever!"

The record books!

There certainly wasn't anything left to say. So, I gave a twitch, bit my nails and sent a prayer into the wild blue yonder.

No more worries!

I think not.

Chapter 4

~ KEEPING SECRETS ~

Waldo Waterman must be turning over in his grave – Orville and Wilbur, too. Nuclear Fusion, raising alligators, homemade airplanes! *Great. Just great.*

That night I took out my pen and added the following to my growing list of worries:

~ WORRY #3 ~

As sure as my name is Winsley Maybeth Walker, If Gramps

doesn't stop talking all this plane nonsense, he's going to get us all in trouble – not just with Hinkle, but with EVERY living soul in Cross Lanes, maybe the entire state of West Virginia, too.

~ WORRY #4 ~

If Gramps does figure out some cock-a-mamie way to get some contraption to FLY, someone might . . . die!

~ WORRY #5 ~

I need to beware of "Little Ole Dimples." She could turn on a dime and her power is mighty because of her big-mouth mama.

Daddy was seldom home, so it was Gramps and Billy who always ended up doing the Mother's Day shopping for Mother and Granny while I baked a cake, and since I was the closest thing we had to an artist in the family, it was also my job to design and make their cards.

This year, Gramps told me to do an extra special job on my part because the gifts might be a bit lacking. Even though he didn't say it was on account of ordering plans for *Emerald Eyes*, I knew it just the same.

I thought my hand-drawn birds and butterflies on both Granny's and Mother's card bordered on the spectacular. Still, I was relieved when Gramps and Billy showed up with two rosebushes to go along with the cards.

That is, until the following Sunday as Granny and Mother were in the midst of hugging everyone for the rosebushes, Billy let things slip when he stated, "Digging 'em up was hard work."

Mother shrieked "What did you just say young man?"

Granny turned pale, reached for her bottle of White Lightning with one hand and whacked off a large piece of chocolate cake with the other.

It took several minutes but when Mother got to the bottom of things, she and Granny were horrified to learn that their presents had, up until that very day, graced the entrance out at *Our Eternal Life* – the cemetery.

Gramps laughed and said, "Don't reckon dead bodies out at *Our Eternal Life* are going to be getting' a whiff of anything, except their own stinkin' decaying bodies."

"That's enough, Dad," Daddy said, looking over at Billy and me.

Gramps continued, "I'm just saying, as for me, I reckon there are bigger and better roses in Heaven . . . but maybe I'm wrong . . . judging by the rest of you."

Between nips, Granny didn't make a lot of sense when she said, "Dust-to-dust, ashes-to-ashes, these here rosebushes are going right back."

Mother stood up and faced Granny. "Well, now, let's think about this. I'm not sure I want to chance putting 'em back. I would die . . . simply die . . . if all of Cross Lanes found out my Mother's Day gift was stolen . . . and from the cemetery, of all places!"

After a long and teary debate, Granny gave in, agreeing the best option was to quietly replant the bushes in our adjoining yards.

Daddy put his arm around Mother's shoulder and said, "Don't worry, honey, those roses are sure to die. Nothing good comes from evil."

I guess he figured it would be some kind of justice if the roses withered away.

Mother made Gramps and Billy wait till nightfall before getting their shovels back out, in case any of the neighbors were looking up the hill toward us.

So, by the light of the moon, both bushes went back in the ground. And wouldn't you know it, in no time at all, thorny bushes that started out looking too scraggly to survive, ended up yielding the most beautiful and glorious roses in all of Cross Lanes.

Mother remarked, "It figures. I should have known those stolen bushes would flourish just to spite me."

"They sure are pretty," I ventured to say one day after I'd made the last red check on my calendar and we were home free for the summer, as Mother and I arranged several tall vases of roses for the church altar.

"Winsley, I want you to know that putting roses on the altar is my little way of honoring the dead out at the cemetery. But make no mistake about it, if you ever tell another living soul about any of this,

I'll be stickin' you head-first in the ground at *Our Eternal Life*. And don't think I won't."

I zipped my lips and threw away the key. "Yes, ma'am."

My lips were sealed but I think Dimples Cheeksly figured things out when her Uncle Fritz died the second week of June. Every time she came over after that, she never failed to mention that something didn't look quite right at the cemetery. Then, she'd fix her eyes on me and pause, as if waiting for me to spill the beans. She made me so nervous I wanted to blurt out the whole truth . . . and nothing but the truth!

Instead, I'd keep sorting my colored art pencils by length as I rattled on about how things were always being switched around for one funeral or another.

As I talked, I pictured a black and white photo in my social studies book. Underneath a sinking ship in the WWII chapter we never got to, the words "Loose Lips Sink Ships" were written across a small lapping wave. It was plain to see that one itty-bitty wave was fixing to destroy a big battleship and dump a million people to the sharks.

The more I thought about that little wave, the louder Mother's words crashed down upon me.

So, I talked . . . and talked . . . and talked some more. Unfortunately, the more I gabbed, the higher one of Dimples's eyebrows always shot up. I knew that eyebrow was her way of letting me know she wasn't buying my story. Even so, I'd chat on, making my ponytail swing back-and-forth as I waved my stubby tangerine-polished nails this-way-and-that, hoping to distract her.

It must have worked. She never told. Of course, for all I know, it could have been the unspoken promise of a free plane ride that kept me safe from the sharks.

Throughout one of our conversations, I lost count of all the times I bent to pick up a stubby little green pencil. Every time I put it back on my nightstand, it would roll slowly to the edge and crash to the floor.

The name "Leprechaun Green" was printed neatly across it. It was hard not to wonder how close the hue of that little pencil came to the color of eyes one would call "emerald."

Maybe Dimples and the good people of Cross Lanes were right. Maybe we were all half-crazy. And maybe, I should just toss that mean little pencil in the trash and never look back. Or maybe I shouldn't even try to stop Gramps and grab my life-jacket to save myself.

Chapter 5

~ Little Brick House ~

~ Worry #6 ~

WE'RE going to disappear from the face-of-the-earth . . . or move 30 minutes down the road.
No difference – not really.

Toward the end of June on a Saturday, several things happened all at once. The blueprints arrived. Mother grounded Billy from his go-cart, and my twitch jumped from part-time to full.

Since I was helping Granny wash out canning jars, I never really knew exactly why Billy was punished in the first place. It might have been for smoking corn-silk cigarettes in someone's shed or for a couple of figure eights through prize-winning flower beds. I imagine you could pretty much take your pick from a jillion things.

After I left Granny and arrived back home, I asked what happened but Daddy only muttered, "He's all boy, that's what."

As usual, Daddy was on his way out the door to tinker under the hood of the car and could afford to shrug it off.

It was Mother who was always apologizing to neighbors for trodden-down tomato plants or picking up a ball from bits of broken glass that used to be someone's living room window. I guess it only stands to reason that she took things a little harder than Daddy.

With Daddy occupied and Billy in his room, I thought all the hoopla was over. But boy was I wrong.

In no time at all, came soft tapping on Billy's bedroom window. Gramps. Luckily, Mother had her head under her big tent hair dryer and didn't have a clue.

Just as soon as Billy cracked the window open, Gramps beckoned. "Hop on out."

"Can't. I'm grounded," Billy answered.

"Sure you can. Come on, let's go."

With a grin and a shrug, Billy climbed out and disappeared from sight.

I wasn't in the mood to tattle. The way I saw it, traipsing around the neighborhood with Gramps wasn't likely to get either of them killed. Besides, I wasn't the one who did the grounding or constantly had my head under a louder-than-an-explosion hair dryer.

Book in hand, I headed for the only place where I could be alone – the bathroom. I slung a quilt and pillow in the bathtub and climbed in.

Determined to finish reading *Building Your Dream Machine,* I'd much rather have been on the train to New York with Jo March in *Little Women.* Unfortunately, I needed to learn all that I could about how stupid airplanes were constructed if I was going to have a shot at battling the building of one.

An hour later and half-way through the chapter about rudders, the screech of "Billy Ray Walker, you get on home . . . RIGHT NOW!" brought my reading to a complete halt.

I jumped out of the tub, wrapped a towel around me and flew down the hall toward Billy's open bedroom window.

Outside, Billy and Gramps were ambling up the

hill. Billy had an ice-cream cone in one hand and what looked to be an old windshield from a motorcycle in the other. I could only pray it was from the junkyard and not from a patron down at the Blue Parrot, our one and only local beer joint.

Mother continued to rant. "Billy, you git on in here. And I mean RIGHT NOW, young man."

Just so Gramps would know someone was keeping an eye on the plane progress, I yelled out the window. "Some windshield you've got there. Looks awfully old and too scratched up to see through. Doubt it would do to be part of anybody's plane."

Gramps laughed and yelled back, "It'll do."

About that time, Mother screamed "Billy" again. Instead of speeding up, Billy merely handed the windshield to Gramps and continued to lollygag up the hill.

Mother flew toward me and demanded to know why I didn't stop Billy from sneaking off in the first place. "Why didn't you tell me your brother left his room? You knew he was being punished!"

"Sorry," I answered, sliding past her.

I made it to the kitchen just as Billy waltzed through the door.

Mother was so close behind me, she nearly knocked me down when I skidded to a stop.

Ice-cream was melting faster than Billy could lick. Plops splattered on the floor.

"Billy, you are in trouble . . . BIG TROUBLE," Mother said, fire in her eyes.

"Sorry," Billy muttered, popping the bottom of the cone in his mouth.

"Sorry isn't good enough, young man." Mother ran water over a dishtowel before handing it to Billy. "Clean up this mess."

To Billy's credit, he didn't blame his partner in crime. He merely bent down and wiped up dots of ice cream as he tried to lick what remained on his chin.

Mother added, "When you're done, go to your room and don't you DARE come out until you memorize a verse!"

Later that evening after Mother calmed down, she smiled as Billy recited Psalm 26:32: "I praise the Lord for keeping me from slipping and falling."

I was tempted to remind Mother it was the same verse he always recited and one of the shortest in the Bible. But I didn't. Nor did I mention the fact that Billy spent the afternoon eating an entire bag of gummy worms while he washed tiny toy cars in a big bowl of soapy water.

Thanks to Gramps, Billy's miniature car collection was growing by leaps and bounds right in front of Mother's eyes and no one seemed to notice but me. I guess when it comes to Billy, so much for "toys need to be earned" and "candy rots your teeth."

Mother had Billy say his slippin' and fallin' verse again at the table when we said the blessing. I wanted to laugh out loud but pretended to have a coughing fit instead. More than likely, Billy was thankful he hadn't slipped or fallen on his way out his bedroom window, as he shimmied down to the ground where Gramps was waiting for him.

No doubt Daddy caught on, too. He was trying not to laugh along with me. Between fake-sounding coughs, he sputtered, "Emmie, water."

"No rain in the forecast," Mother answered.

"I mean . . . water to drink."

"There's the sink," Mother shot back.

Now, some of my friends had sickeningly sweet mothers. They were the kind of mothers who never raised their voices and seemed to float through life baking cookies and smiling at the West Virginia sunsets.

My mother wasn't that kind. She was spunky. Maybe it was her instinct for survival, living next door to her in-laws and all, that gave her grit. Or maybe she was born that way. I don't know.

I do know that she was trying really hard to raise Billy to be a good and decent person while all of Cross Lanes watched. Mother was determined that, as Methodist, we couldn't let the Baptists think we were inferior in any way, shape or form. She often summed-up in one word what she didn't want us to be – heathens. The reason I knew all of this was because she told us so – repeatedly.

To Mother's credit, nothing more was said about Billy's afternoon escape until after the dinner dishes had been washed, rinsed and dried.

After I put away the last pot, I went looking for Mother. I intended to tell her I was sorry about not keeping a better watch on Billy. Mother and Daddy were in their bedroom with the door shut. I sat down in the hallway, my ear pressed to the bedroom door.

Every so often, I caught phrases like "tired of these shenanigans" and "downright ornery" and "not talking about Billy, this time."

Things sounded simple. Mother wanted Daddy to tell Gramps that she was the boss in her own house and that he, Gramps, better remember it in the future – especially before prying open bedroom windows or such stuff.

Then she continued. "Will, I'm serious. It's not fair every time I try to discipline our child my authority is undermined by your father. Billy needs to know there are rules and limits."

"Dad does tend to spoil him, but he doesn't mean to upset you, Emmie."

"Will, listen to me. We've got an eight-year-old who doesn't mind a word I say. This time, I mean business. You've got to make it clear to that old man or we're moving. Understand?"

I imagined that Daddy had started to squirm, because Mother's voice never softened – not once.

"Emmie, you know Dad don't mean no harm."

"Oh, by the way, I'd thought I'd call to see if that cute red brick house we saw on the way to Charleston is still on the market," Mother answered.

With that, Mother had thrown down the gauntlet.

The light shifted in the hallway, and I realized too late the door had opened and both of my parents were now staring down at me.

"Winsley, whatever are you doing?" Mother asked.

"I dropped my ring and it rolled down the hallway," I fibbed.

Slyly, I slid a ring off my finger as I stood up. I opened my clinched fist and held out my little birthstone ring.

Complete silence.

Mother threw "Goodness. For a second there, I thought you were eavesdropping," over her shoulder as she walked away.

My heart fluttered. Mother knew more than I thought. *Drats.* I'd have to be more careful in the future.

Daddy kissed Mother on her forehead as he went out the kitchen door. As usual, he meandered toward my grandparents' house. I, of course, followed. The only thing different this evening from all the times before, was that in order to get inside the door, Dad had to squeeze sideways between growing stacks of soon-to-be airplane parts that lined the porch.

I slipped in the house behind him and hid in the kitchen. From there, I could hear every word being spoken in the living room to the beat of the soft clicks of Granny's knitting needles.

For a while the three grown-ups talked about next-to-nothing until Daddy said, "Emmie's hankering to move closer to town."

The clicking stopped.

Dead silence.

Finally, Granny said, "Well, son, you know the Undertakers moved from some place in northern Ohio before they moved down to Charleston and then ended up here. And frankly, they're thought of as gypsies by many Cross Lanes folks, even today."

Daddy answered, "Oh for heaven sakes! I hardly think a move thirty minutes down the road would qualify us as gypsies. Honestly, Mom."

"I'm just saying you don't want to get into the habit of roaming from one place to another. Now, do you? People need to stay put, if you ask me."

After clearing his throat, Gramps chimed in, "Sure would hate to see you go, even if is just thirty miles down the road."

I figured this was as good as an apology from Gramps, or at least, as close to one as we were likely to get.

Confirmation for that came when the conversation moved on to the fact that the birds were having a heyday eating all Granny's green tomatoes before she could get them off the vine and fried.

I yawned and headed home after Granny said, "The drainage ditch down by the road is holdin' water bad. We need to get the weeds cleaned out before mosquitoes eat us alive."

A while later Daddy walked in with a smile on his face. I heard him reassure Mother that he'd reached an understanding with Gramps. In a way, I guess he had. Daddy let it be known that Mother would force a move if things got worse and Gramps said he'd hate to see us go.

Of course, if you were a good listener – which I was, Gramps didn't really promise anything.

Still, the calm that followed would lure Mother into thinking she had won.

As for Billy, it seemed a short Bible verse and a quick "I'm sorry" were all it took to get him off the hook. But knowing Mother like I did, I could tell she was never all that taken-in with Daddy's version of Gramps's could-be apologies.

At the end of the day, I was worn out. There hadn't been any ice cream for me, no new toy or candy either, just a big heap of worry that wouldn't go away.

As I thought about it all, I drew colored blobs on a piece of paper with my art pencils. After discarding several possibilities, I circled a big lavender blob – the exact shade of purple I wanted on the walls of my new bedroom, the one in the little brick house.

No one else seemed to know it yet, but if things continued as they were, I figured we were as good as thirty minutes down the road, ten by air.

Chapter 6

~ Blind Bates ~

~ WORRY #7 ~

IF I don't KEEP MY EYE
On tHE ball,
I'M going to End uP a
CHURCH uMPiRE.
PHOOEY on tHat!

The pile of airplane parts-to-be on Gramps's driveway seemed to multiply like the weeds in Granny's mid-summer okra patch. Luckily, the more rusted and dented the stuff looked, the slower my twitch and fewer the butterflies.

At the end of July, Gramps and Billy came home from the junkyard looking like grease-monkeys and smelling like rubber tires. As they unloaded several boxes of bolts, hinges and metal tubing, Gramps said, "Be on the prowl for a rubber hose, Billy boy."

I knew Billy had accomplished his mission the following Saturday when Daddy yelled in through our screen door, "Where in tarnation is the blasted hose? Don't know how anyone expects me to wash the car without it."

What Billy didn't know was I'd completed my mission, too.

When no one was looking, I'd swiped the hose right back from Gramps' driveway, and a couple of metal pipes – to boot. Now, they were stuffed in the back of my closet. I figured when it came to stopping Gramps, everything was fair game.

After a few more choice words and a bit of stomping around, Daddy yelled again, "If that hose doesn't show up in a minute or two, well . . . then . . . I reckon I've got me a free afternoon."

With that, Dad was back inside flipping through the channels faster than the screen door had a chance to slam behind him. After more clicks than I could count, he finally landed on *Handyman Fix-it.*

Since I was in the middle of sorting family photos on the floor of the den, I learned how to fix a leaky faucet alongside him.

As the two of us watched, I got to thinking about the water situation over at Granny's and how the whole thing came to be.

Years ago, Gramps bought two acres of land; one for him and one for us.

At the time, Mother said, "Giving your son a plot of land is one thing. Having that land buttin' up against yours is another."

"Either this or nothin' I guess," Daddy said as he plucked a puny-looking plum from a scraggly-looking tree on the very spot where our house was to be built.

As he handed Mother the plum, she said, "Cryin' shame."

Daddy may have thought Mother's comment was about plowing down the plum tree but I figured she was talking about living next door to her in-laws.

Either way, two foundations were poured and Gramps and Daddy began to hammer away.

They did it all – except for the plumbing, which was contracted out to "Blind Bates."

Later, I said to Gramps, "Seems mean-spirited for people to call a man 'Blind'".

Gramps replied, "Like they say, if the name fits."

"What do you mean?"

"People at the Methodist church can be real unforgiving when it comes to their annual softball tournament. And anyway, he should have made sure his foot touched the base. Now, isn't that right, Winnie-girl?"

"Guess so," I muttered.

Gramps could say whatever he wanted, but it was evident giving Blind the plumbing job was an act of Christianity, rather than necessity. Everyone knew Blind was living from hand-to-mouth and not doing a very good job of it, at that.

When Blind finished both of our houses, it was determined we fared better than Granny and Gramps.

Every time Gramps turned on the faucet in the kitchen, the toilet down the hall flushed. Spit and loud cussing would swirl all over Granny's otherwise immaculate, sunny yellow kitchen. Even so, Gramps refused to get Blind back to fix things. He said, "Sure don't want to risk the situation getting worse."

Granny felt otherwise. "Seth, I'm begging you, get Blind back – and soon!"

"Woman, for the life of me, I can't imagine why you'd want that. If you ask me, it'd be like the double whammy, for sure."

With a tad firmer voice, Granny answered, "Well, I'd hate to think for the rest of my life every time I flush the toilet, our washing machine is going to jump to life."

Since their rattlely machine already practically

walked across the linoleum floor whenever Granny chanced to wash, Gramps must have known he was defeated.

He reached for the phone.

Blind came back.

Gramps was right.

It was the double whammy.

From that day on, whenever Gramps tried to get a drink from the sink, not only did the toilet flush, but water also gushed out of the garden hose.

In the end, Granny resorted to keeping a pitcher of ice water handy on the kitchen counter which seemed to do the trick. Gramps could help himself to a drink of water. Granny wouldn't have to pray for the forgiveness of his foul language, and the toilet stayed quiet.

Frankly, I thought it was a stroke of genius on her part and could well imagine Granny building an airplane without any blueprints to go by.

One day as the two of us washed apples in the kitchen sink, I said this very thing to her.

She replied, "Well, see here, Winsley girl, you know I can't start on no airplane until I get these apples made into butter."

I laughed.

She winked.

And that was the end of that.

Chapter 7

~ Dimples, Farley and the Runaway ~

~ Worry #8 ~

The Bookmobile will pass

me by – or pull up empty.

P.S. I need food, shelter, clothing

. . . and books to live!

Gramps now parked in the grass due to the ev-er-growing number of boxes of soon-to-be airplane parts scattered from one end of his driveway to the other.

"Don't you dare park that car within a foot of my roses," Granny said, shaking her finger in his face on more than one occasion.

Again, being the ornery person that he was, Gramps continued to speed up the driveway and zoom toward the roses. He'd skid to a stop mere inches away.

"I'll solve that," Granny muttered as she thrust her garden shears deep into her rosebush. Afterwards, roses filled every vase and canning jar Granny owned, even her good punch bowl overflowed with them. And whenever a rose looked puny or lost its petals, Granny just headed outside for more.

Upon entering the house one day, Gramps said, "The place smells like a funeral parlor. Thought stolen flowers were supposed to wither up and die away."

"You hesh up," Granny answered. "I'll tell you what I DON'T want, and that's to stumble through a maze of boxes every time I walk out my door. And . . . to tell you the truth, I'm startin' to get weary of all of that airplane talk."

I was surprised to hear Granny say that. No one, but no one, ever mentioned the airplane anymore – except Gramps . . . and me, of course.

Oh, occasionally, I'd hear a neighbor or someone say, "What's all that stuff for, Seth?"

To which he'd answer, "Goin' build me an air-o-plane."

Afterwards, laughter would ring out and that would be the last of it.

I wanted to tug on everyone's sleeve and yell "Wake up, people. He's not kidding. Can't you see what's happening?"

Even if I did, I doubt anyone would bother coming to my rescue. So, I did what I always did to escape. I read.

Kids in Cross Lanes had a couple of options if they wanted to read during the summer months.

The first was to beg your parents to make the long drive to Charleston. The problem was most families only owned one car, and transportation to work took higher priority than a trip to the library.

Another option was to trade books with your friends. Well, whoop-de-doo. I'd already read everything for miles around that I could get my hands on.

Luckily, a third option chugged into town once a week and parked on the lot at Grayson's Grocery: the Kanawha Valley Bookmobile! *God Bless the Bookmobile!*

On Bookmobile Day, I'd hang around the swivel rack of cosmetics near the window in the grocery store, doing my best to look like I was on the verge of spending a wad on powder and paint, as Granny called it.

Even though the store was always deserted, Mr.

Grayson never failed to make his point. "You a paying customer or not?"

I'd give a little nod and keep on twirling the cosmetic rack this-way-and-that. But as soon as I heard the distant whine of the Bookmobile's engine, I'd dart out the door.

My tactic for being first-in-line never failed since that old dilapidated bus always arrived at the exact same time every Thursday.

You'd think most kids would know that and get themselves a head start toward it. Instead, it seemed they waited until it came to a stop and the door groaned open. Then, there'd be a loud stampede along with a lot of dull thuds, as books were dropped helter-skelter.

Behind me, kids jostled and elbowed each other in an attempt to move up in line. By the time I reached the top step, what started out as a mild rumbling would now be an ear-splitting roar as twelve to fifteen kids shouted at me to hurry it up.

The fact that Mr. Farley only allowed in two kids at a time didn't matter to me, I'd waited all week and I was determined to choose wisely, and that took time. Lots of time.

Not only did Mr. Farley drive the Bookmobile, he also stamped the due date on our books. Why he bothered, I don't know. Books were always due back the following Thursday when he rumbled through town again.

I lived in fear Mr. Farley would skip Cross

Lanes or take us off the list forever. Books were the only thing that took my mind off my worry list. Books were a necessity to me, and I needed Farley and his old Bookmobile. And for that very reason, I always forced myself to be nice to him.

I hopped up the steps and through the yellow door. "Hello, Mr. Farley. How are you, today?"

"Doin' fair, Winsley, 'cept for a little bout of stiff shoulder."

His ailments changed, but our conversation usually stayed pretty much the same.

"Sorry to hear that."

"Rained last night and every time it does, my joints stiffen up. Can't be helped, I guess."

"Guess not," I answered.

"How's Seth doing?" he questioned. "Heard he was building himself an airplane."

I decided to ignore his airplane comment. "Gramps is fine. Said to tell you to stop in for a bushel of apples. We're pickin' more than we can eat."

"Your Granny makin' apple butter?"

"You bet. Morning, noon and night."

"Tell Seth and Birdie I'll make it a point to stop by after Prayer Meeting on Wednesday."

"I'll do that . . . but Granny said anyone wantin' butter gotta bring their own jars. She's given away so much of the stuff she barely has any jars left."

Outside, the chanting and stomping was reaching fever pitch. Some goober was even pounding on the side of the bus. That didn't hurry me along but the fact that the bus was getting stuffy did. I grabbed every book that had "airplane" or the something to do with transportation on its spine. Unfortunately, there weren't all that many.

As Farley stamped my books, I took a deep breath and pulled a folded piece of paper from my pocket and handed it to him.

He glanced at it before saying, "Okay, I'll try to find it, but you gotta remember I can't bring a book if it's already checked out from the main branch."

"Thanks, Mr. Farley. I'm dying to read *Jo's Boys*. Did you know it's a sequel to *Little Women?*"

As always, Farley, Defender of the Books, got the last word, "No, but I'll tell you one thing I do know, and that is you'd better remember people gotta pay for any lost or damaged books. New ones ain't cheap to replace and your family already had to pay for one, if memory serves me right."

"That happened three years ago when Billy was only five years old. He didn't know any better. Besides, Daddy paid in full as if the book was brand new – which it WASN'T."

"Don't matter. Still on the record," Farley answered as he handed me my books and reached for Dimples Cheeksly's pile.

Mr. Farley gave Dimples a big smile and she gave him one right back. Of course, he had a smile for her. One of her brothers was in Seminary and the other just got tapped to lead a small church over in Red House. No scribbled-in, chewed-up old book on her record.

Farley handed me my books.

I let out a sigh.

Dimples gave me a pity smile.

Sure, she could afford to throw some little smile my way and stand there looking all superior.

Even so, I wasn't about to let Dimples know her good standing with Farley was a thorn in my side. I stuck out my tongue and flounced away.

I clutched my books tightly to my chest. Twelve was the limit. I'd have to read like a snail, or read them over and over again to make them last the whole week.

Maybe it was a good thing Farley didn't know there were far more bothersome things on Billy's "record" than some scribbling in an old copy of *The Pokey Little Puppy*.

Kids still waiting in the hot sun cheered as Farley opened the door to let me out and someone else in.

I stuck my tongue out at the whole lot of them and skipped triumphantly away. After all, I had *Little House on the Prairie* among the boring airplane books in my hands.

Even though Dimples Cheeksly was annoying at times, she was the only other kid around who understood about reading and books, and stuff like that.

We might bicker now and then, but as usual

Dimples showed up later that day to play library. We always took turns pretending to be a librarian or Mrs. Caldwell, the prettiest teacher at Cross Lanes Elementary.

Not one to miss things, Dimples said, "Looks like you're up to something with all those books about planes."

"We've never had a nonfiction section before, that's all," I answered with a twitch and a couple of butterfly flutters. "Now who do you want to be . . . some new librarian in town or Mrs. Caldwell?"

As usual, Dimples chose Mrs. Caldwell and I was Nellie Reader, the pretend new librarian in town with seven little pretend kids I had to work long hours to feed.

While I chased my unruly children throughout the library, Dimples was too busy writing lesson plans to worry about all the plane books.

A couple of hours later, my own Mother called from the kitchen, "Wins, is Billy with you?"

Dimples stood up to leave, saying, "Winsley, you really ought to see someone about that tic."

Before I had time to answer either of them, Mother called again. "Go find Billy. Tell him to get washed up."

As soon as Dimples went out the door, I slipped my feet in my flip-flops and followed her out. I found Granny at the clothesline. She handed me the short end of a long tablecloth to help fold.

"You seen Billy, Granny?"

"Not today."

"Think he might be roaming around with Gramps somewhere?"

"Nope. Seth left earlier to take a bushel of apples to Cousin Ollie over in St. Albans. Know for a fact Billy wasn't with him because I ran out with a couple of jars of apple butter as Seth was backing down the driveway."

After handing her the folded tablecloth, I turned toward home. "If you see Billy, tell him supper's ready."

With a clothespin in her mouth, Granny answered. "Sure thing."

Back inside our kitchen, I shrugged when Mother said, "If he can't get himself home in time for dinner, then he can eat what's left or do without."

When Daddy got in from work, he joined Mother and me at the table.

Between bites of cornbread, Daddy said, "I ought to wallop that kid just to get him in gear."

We all laughed but deep down, I was beginning to get an uneasy feeling in the pit of my stomach and my butterflies were starting to act up.

Throughout the meal, Mother kept dropping her spoon. A sure sign she was worried, too.

As soon as the sun dipped below the hills, everything changed. Daddy took off in the car.

In the clear mountain air, we could hear him calling Billy's name as he drove from one end of Cross Lanes to the other.

Mother flipped on lights. I figured she was hoping to draw Billy to the light like a moth or some nasty old bug.

I sat in our porch swing with Granny. Even though she stayed silent, her twisted-up hankie said it all.

Gramps arrived home from St. Albans. He lifted an old dinner bell out of a box on his driveway. "Glad I didn't get around to melting down this thing last summer."

The clank of the bell brought the neighbors. With trembling hands, Mother measured coffee and started the percolator. Fire Chief Knight unfolded a map, handed out flashlights and pointed men in different directions, saying, "Check back no later than midnight! We don't want to have to come lookin' for any of you."

Daddy returned. He grabbed his flashlight and said, "I'll search out back. Planning on checking around the train tracks, too. Don't expect me back until I've had time to walk a mile-or-so in both directions. May take me awhile."

Even though I could barely see straight for the constant twitching of my eye, I followed Daddy around back and watched as he disappeared in the darkness. I tried to calm myself down with the thought if Billy had been kidnapped, the kidnapper would let him go. After all, it was Billy we were talking about.

Before rejoining Mother and Granny around

front, I darted inside to get my worry list and a pencil. Back outside, I couldn't make out all of their words but Granny's half-whispered prayers were soothing nonetheless.

By the glow of the porch light, I flipped to a clean page in my worry notebook and wrote the following:

~ SCARY ~

WHat iF tHE sun wEnt down WHilE BillY was walking in tHE woods And HE can't Find His waY back HOME?

~ SCARIER ~

WHat iF BillY Put a PEnnY on tHE Train tracks a train Hit it, SHooting out His EYEball And HE's wandERing around HalF-blind SOMEWHERE?

~ SCARIEST ~

What if Billy never comes back?

As soon as I put the dot under the last question mark, the ring of the telephone caused us all to jump. I ran inside and dove for the phone, not wanting Mother to hear any bad news firsthand.

At the sound of a squeaky voice, I thought we had a female kidnapper until I recognized my other Granny's voice on the line.

Granny Brown lived in Point Pleasant and never phoned unless someone took sick or a distant relative died. I prayed we weren't looking at a funeral on top of everything else.

"When y'all comin' for the boy?" Granny Brown yelled.

No matter how many times I'd told her she didn't need to yell just because the call was long distance, as usual, she was screaming.

I swallowed hard. "What?"

"When y'all coming for Billy?"

"Is Billy with *you?*"

"Yup, he sure is. And grown an inch since I saw him last. I do declare, an inch or maybe more, for sure."

I wanted to sob for joy. "What's he doing there? How did he get there?"

"Seems he hid on the library bus while Bob Farley was in Grayson's getting a sodee pop. Bob dropped him off here after his last stop over in Poca, saying he was in a hurry and didn't feel inclined to double all the way back to Cross Lanes. I would have called earlier but the line was dead. Some high-flying car took out a pole two miles south of here and the lines have been down."

"Hold on. Mother's gonna want to talk to you," I answered, anxious to spread the word.

Gramps clanked the dinner bell three times. Searchers stumbled toward their homes, most dragging their feet and looking aggravated.

Chief Knight pounded on our back door. "I've cranked up the fire engine on more than one occasion because of Billy Walker and frankly . . . me and everyone else in Cross Lanes is gettin' downright tired of it."

Mother stepped back and gave Daddy a push toward the door.

Now, instead of facing Mother, Chief Knight was eye-to-eye with Daddy.

"Sorry," Daddy muttered.

"That may be good enough for some . . . but not for me. Cross Lanes folks are good folks but there's a line . . . and frankly, your son has stepped over it. WAY OVER."

I hoped Daddy would slam the door in Chief Knight's face. Instead, he said, "Other than the fact that Wally Undertaker sprained his ankle tripping over a croquet wicket, I thought everything went as well as could be expected."

Chief Knight stared him down.

Daddy added, "Uh . . . uh . . .uh . . . under the circumstances, of course."

Chief Knight must have been at a loss for words because he turned and walked away without saying another word.

Since Daddy had to get up for work at five in the morning, we piled in the car without even taking the time to turn out the lights.

For the forty-five minutes it took from our driveway to pull up at Granny Brown's, Mother talked about how she couldn't bear to live without her baby, her Billy. She brought up the poor Lindberg baby and repeated over and over that the poor little thing was found buried in a shallow grave, and in his own yard, mind you.

After a bunch of hellos, hugs and goodbyes, the ride home turned into an entirely different matter. Instead of crying for her little lost baby, Mother was rip-roaring mad at Billy for worrying the whole lot of Cross Lanes "plum near crazy."

"Whatever were you thinking?" Mother demanded to know.

"Gramps needs a throttle for his airplane and I thought there was one in Granny Brown's old shed."

"What would make you think you find one there, of all places? You know you're not supposed to be in there – too many sharp tools and things laying around." Daddy looked back at Billy in his rearview mirror.

Billy shrugged.

Mother turned toward Daddy and said, "Will, are you listening to me? Mark my words, that crazy airplane your dad keeps talking about is going to be the death of someone!"

"Well, now, baby . . . that plane ain't built yet. Let's not get all carried away."

"Carried away? If you ask me, someone NEEDS to get carried away and put a stop to this nonsense!" Mother screamed.

Daddy ended the conversation when he answered, "It's late, let's not worry about it any more tonight."

I forgave Billy when he pulled *Jo's Boys* out from under his shirt.

"How'd you get this?" I whispered in the dark.

"Someone in Poca checked it in and the old coot shelved it."

I smiled and pulled Billy close. He didn't resist and in no time at all, was sound asleep.

I couldn't wait to tell Dimples I was going to be the first one in Cross Lanes to read *Jo's Boys*. I seriously doubted either one of her brothers would stoop to swipe a book for her! I'd worry about turning in thirteen books, instead of the allowed twelve, next Thursday and not a minute sooner.

God had answered my prayers and thrown in a good book, to boot. *Hallelujah!*

If I'd had a pencil with me, I would have scratched off Worry #2, the one about having to move out of West Virginia because of Billy. I figured if he left, we'd all want to go with him – no matter what.

Not by air, of course, but with him . . . just the same.

Chapter 8

~ Unexpected Delivery ~

~ Worry #9 ~

On a Balance Scale,

If these were on one side:

Tornado, Fire, Lightning,

Earthquake, Hurricane,

and Gramps, Billy, & the Plane

WERE on the other side, the scale would be tipped toward GRaMPS, Billy and the Plane WHEN it COMES to the amount of Damage LEFt BEHind.

My twitch slowed and the butterflies left when Dimples quit yakking about the missing cemetery roses and then, all but came to a stop when Farley didn't bother to count my return books the following week. At this rate, I'd be able to start sixth grade like everyone else – happy and free.

The first day of school was less than two weeks away. Back-to-school at my house meant the whir of the sewing machine. Although Mother tried steering me toward bolts of dark-colored cotton in Fanny's Fabrics earlier in the week, I kept inching back toward the pinks and lavenders. When Mother finally relented and asked for a yard of the lavender stripe, I thought maybe we had reached a real turning point.

Yes, life was good:

Car problems occupied Gramps.

Billy left for Scout Camp.

Mother was tethered to the sewing machine.

Daddy was working the "Hoot Owl" shift and the two of us ate pancakes for an entire week – his breakfast, my dinner.

I was as close to living worry-free as I'd ever been in my entire life.

Unfortunately, no sooner had I laid *Homemade Airplanes for Flying Americans* aside and squirreled Mother's well-worn copy of *Gone with the Wind* from her nightstand, everything slipped back to normal and life was . . . well, *life*.

"Hoot Owl" turned to "Day" and pancakes turned to Brussel Sprouts.

Billy returned from camp with a badge for whittling and now my bedposts were taking on the look of totem poles. Except for a loud backfire every couple miles or so, Gramps' car was up and running.

Mother needed more ric-rac and borrowed Gramps's car for a second trip to Fanny's. I didn't go. Now, I was looking at a host of plaids – mainly brown, navy and dark green. *Great.* And of course, more ric-rac. *Double Great.*

Worse, the minute Gramps's car troubles were gone, he grabbed hold of the blueprints for old *Emerald Eyes* and didn't let go. Just the sight of that rolled up paper under his arm meant my twitch was back. The butterflies, too.

If for no other reason than my health, I had to put a stop to all of airplane nonsense, and decided to enlist Granny's help. I cornered her one morning as she was dividing a sink-full of pink roses into small bunches.

"What'cha doing, Granny?"

"Fixin' to take flowers to the unknowns out at *Our Eternal Life*," Granny said as she slid a knife along a stem like she was buttering a piece of toast. Thorns dove into the sink as if looking for cover.

The "unknowns" was Granny's name for the dead beneath weather-worn tombstones so crumbly you couldn't read their names

"PINK, Granny? Why Pink?" I asked.

She shrugged.

She didn't seem to care if the recipient of her PINK flowers was a "he" or a "she" but it seemed wrong to me. Before I got a chance to mention that Mother's red roses were on the spurt again and we could use those for the "unknowns", Granny handed me a spool of pink ribbon and said, "Winsley-girl, give me a hand makin' the bows."

"Granny, how about using some other color — at least for the bows? Pink is for girls. I doubt some dead man would want to look down from heaven to find pink roses with a pink-checked bow lying across his grave."

"Heavens, child, these people are dead. What do they care? Not likely they're going to be ooohing and aaahing over some roses — no matter what color. Besides, there's work for people to be doing in heaven. None of those people may have time to figure out where they were laid to rest down here. It's the living that counts, not the dying-part."

"But Granny, you never met these people. Who knows what they liked, what they cared about, or even where they came from, for that matter."

Granny tied another bow before answering, "Be it castle, cottage or caravan, they're all gettin' roses today. Pink ones at that, Missy."

I took a deep breath and blurted out what was really on my mind. "Granny, I'm worried about Gramps and all of that talk about an airplane. Aren't you?"

"Mercy me . . . is that what's causing that ugly tic of yours?" Granny patted my shoulder. "You've gotta stop all that worrying. Hear? And now, fetch me something to put all these glorious arrangements in."

"Where? Every box on the driveway is full to the brim. Besides, they're all soggy from the dew."

Granny frowned. "Oh, good grief. I forgot."

"Bet you're getting mighty tired of boxes all over the driveway."

"Well, I must admit they were a bit of an annoyance at first . . . but now I hardly notice. Guess I've gotten used to them. Reckon I can use Billy's old wagon for my trip to the cemetery. Easier on my back than carrying a box anyway."

After I retrieved Billy's wagon, I tried one last time. "Aren't you 'fraid Gramps will get hurt flying some rickety old plane?"

"I don't think about it much. Besides, remember a couple years ago when flies were bad in Cross Lanes? It looked like we had a plague descent. Your Grandfather had Venus Flytraps lined up from here-to-there and back again."

"What's that got to do with building an airplane?"

"He got tired of those Venus Flytraps and I reckon he'll get tired of trying to put an airplane together, too."

Even though Granny had a way of making things right, I hardly thought throwing out a bunch of dead plants compared to getting tired of building an airplane. Still, I nodded as we made room for the last of the flowers.

Granny put on her sunbonnet and picked up the wagon's rusty handle.

With a quick smile, she said, "I'm off, tou-da-lou."

I watched as Granny walked away, pulling a wagon full of stolen roses back to where they came from in the first place. Only this time, they'd be plopped on the graves of a bunch of people she never knew – not even whether they were man, woman, or child.

As she disappeared from sight, I had a sick feeling in the pit of my stomach. I was on my own when it came to putting a stop to the airplane. My big problem was I still didn't have a clue how to do it.

I headed back inside, thinking about roses and airplanes as I tidied up Granny's kitchen. I was scooping the last of the thorns out of the sink when someone knocked at the front door.

Since it was common for the people of Cross Lanes to give a little whistle and walk on in, I was curious to see who it was that felt the need to stop and knock.

I cracked the door and there in the shadowy doorway stood a tall stranger holding a clipboard in his hand. Behind him loomed a large delivery truck in the driveway.

"Special Delivery for Seth Walker," the man said.

I replied, "He's not here."

The man peered through the screen at me. "Well, someone's gotta sign for it."

"Sign for what?" I asked.

"Well . . . now . . . let me see," he answered, thumbing through papers on his clipboard.

I darted past him and ran to take a peek in the back of the truck. There sat the biggest box I'd ever seen!

The box was bigger than Billy. And bigger than me. In fact, it was almost as big as Gramps, himself.

I jumped up on the truck to read the words printed around on the far side.

It was then I knew my biggest worry had come true. Disaster had literally come knocking on our door.

I climbed down and did my best to look like I was on the verge of tears which wasn't hard, because I was. "He's dead."

The delivery man looked up from his papers. "What's that?"

"Seth Walker. He's dead. Died almost a week ago. Choked on a chicken bone."

The man quit shuffling papers. "Oh, my gaw-sh."

My eyes were watery.

Silence.

I squeezed out one tear – a teeny-tiny one.

More silence.

I squeezed out another one from my other eye.

The delivery man cleared his throat. "Word travels fast around these parts. Seems mighty strange I didn't hear nothin' about a chicken-bone choking . . . are you sure?"

"I'm sure. I'm the one who was sittin' across from him at the table."

"You poor thing," the delivery man replied.

I nodded. "I'm okay . . . but we're all sad, of course."

"Well . . . uh . . . what happened? I mean . . . you hear about things like this . . . but it's hard to imagine exactly HOW it happened."

"Well . . . uh . . . after his usual quick prayer, Gramps said, "Pass the victuals and be quick about it. I'm starving."

Then, my Granny said, "Slow down there, Seth. You're gonna choke to death in front of us all, if'n you don't."

The delivery man replied, "And . . . then what?"

"Well . . . uh . . . then . . . Gramps scooped more

than his share of tators and plopped them on his plate and then, he . . . uh . . . nearly emptied out the gravy boat. Then he . . . uh . . . grabbed a drumstick and yanked off a big bite. Next thing I knowned, he took a bite, clutched his throat, and toppled down."

The delivery man shook his head. "That is awful, just awful."

"That's not the worst of it. Gramps's face landed smack-dab in the middle of his plate. Mashed potatoes and gravy flew across the room like they were late for a date. I had to leave the table without so much as a bite to eat. Mama told me to wash the potatoes out of my hair before they hardened up. I tell you, it took several shampoos to get all that greasy gravy out. The whole thing was one big mess, one big mess." I looked back at the huge box. "Yep, one BIG MESS."

"You don't say." The man placed his pencil behind his ear. "Sure didn't read nothing about any of this in the paper and I didn't hear anything about it in town."

"You know how it is. A person is here one day and gone the next. Speaking of being gone, I 'spect you best be going. Probably got more deliveries to make."

"Ummm . . . well ahhh . . . goodbye then," the man answered as he climbed back into his truck.

I danced a jig on the other side of the screen door as the truck trundled down the driveway.

Ten minutes later, I'd just put the spool of left-over pink ribbon back in Granny's sewing drawer when I heard the whine of an engine and a couple of car doors.

Through the screen door, a familiar voice boomed. "Well, who in the heck would tell such an outlandish tale? I've never been sick a day in my life. Besides, we had pork chops and lima beans last Sunday. "

I couldn't make out the muffled answer but I didn't need to.

I wanted to fall face-first in a mountain of mashed potatoes and let gravy rain on my head. No such luck.

No, my luck was to be the one facing sixth grade with a twitch faster than I could talk and worse, I'd be decked out in plaid from head-to-toe with a bunch of butterflies marching in my stomach. If all that that wasn't bad enough, I'd be wearing enough ric-rac to make everyone on the planet their own personal jump rope.

I might as well go home, throw a teepee over my bedposts, and crawl in. And never, ever come back out. Certainly not for any Sunday dinner.

Chapter 9

~ Outside Little Egypt ~

~ Worry #10 ~

A weekend in the country,

What could possibly go wrong?

EVERYTHING!

That's what.

The last weekend, the one before the beginning of school, didn't happen like all the other weekends that summer. It's harder still to believe the whole bunch of us didn't get arrested. One thing for sure, after that, there was no denying I came from a family of crackpots, liars and thieves. Worse still, I was beginning to be one of them.

In the beginning, things started out like they usually did. If life had a pattern, ours must've been plaid, its lines running this way and that, crossing one another every chance they got. Weekends in the country proved to be no exception.

Summer months when the weather was nice, Gramps and Granny would load up the car on Friday afternoon and head toward their little summer farm back of Red House. It was rare that Billy wasn't along, which meant I had to go, too.

Mother always said, "Winsley-baby, I'm countin' on you to keep an eye on Billy for me."

Truth be known, I had very little control over Billy but I always nodded as if I did.

When I was younger, I thought my grandparents wanted Billy and me along for the pleasure of our company. As I grew older, came the realization that wasn't the case. It was to their benefit to have us there. We were cheap labor.

Upon arriving at the farm on Fridays, Billy and I would unpack the car as Gramps tinkered with his old John Deere. For the longest time, the tractor would sputter and spurt and sound like it would never start, much less move. Eventually, it would jump to life and Gramps would ride out of the barn with a huge grin on his face. "Yes, siree! She's a goodun," he'd shout at the top of his lungs to no one in particular before climbing down.

As usual, the minute Gramps got off, Billy scampered up. I'd pray Gramps would demand that he'd get back down. Of course, Gramps never did. Instead, he'd holler as he entered the house, "Tell Cousin Willie we're here."

Billy would thrust the gear into "Drive." The tractor would lunge. And before Billy and the tractor rumbled away, I'd sprint across the yard and jump up on the back hitch. As I grasped the back of Billy's metal seat, I'd shout in his ear he'd better go slow or I'd tell Mother this time, for sure.

Out of the yard and onto the road we'd bounce. There was seldom a car, so we'd ride down the middle of the road. Since I didn't want to brush against briers and twigs all the way there and back, that was fine with me, too.

In ten to fifteen minutes, we'd pull up to Gramps's cousin's house and shout through the screen door that Gramps and Granny were here for the weekend. From the shadows, Cousin Willie's answer was always the same. "Alrighty, then." And that would be the last we'd see or hear from him until the following Friday when we bounced through his yard and up to the screen door again. To make the trip worthwhile, we'd fill our pockets with apples on our way out of Cousin Willie's yard – ones we could reach as we trundled by and whatever was free for the picking.

Being in the country was the opposite of being at home. For one thing, there wasn't a television at the farm. So, Billy played with toys and I'd drag out Gramps's old set of McGuffey readers to thumb-through until dark. After that, the two of us usually tried to catch a couple of fireflies before Granny called us in for bed.

Now Saturday, that was a different matter. It was a day of work which only varied according to the season. In the spring, we'd plant seeds, and in the summer and fall, we'd tend to the crops and harvest them.

Sunday was the Holy Day. No work. This was the way it always was; that is, until the weekend before I started sixth grade. The one where everything went downhill faster than any twitch.

This particular Saturday evening, as the sun dipped below the mountains, and I was working on some arithmetic problems in a McGuffey, I realized I hadn't heard a peep from Billy for the past couple of problems or so.

After a bit of searching, I found Billy in the barn with Gramps. The two of them were hooking up a small trailer to the back of Gramps' car. Once that was done, they opened the trailer doors and threw in a seat from someone's riding mower, the steering wheel from an old car and three tires.

My heart sank.

That heap of junk wouldn't be good for anything . . . except a homemade airplane.

Silently, I left the barn, hoping once Granny knew, she'd put a stop to it.

I searched and found Granny outside washing her hair by the water well. I yelled, but Granny couldn't understand a word I said.

Guess frustration made me flat-out lose my mind because I went inside, picked up the phone and called the police.

"I want to report a burglary here . . . uh . . . here . . . in Red House," I stammered.

"In Red House? Are you sure?" A lady's voice asked, sounding puzzled.

"Yes, ma'am. A burglary."

"Is the burglar still there – in the house?"

"No," I answered, praying Granny would stay outside forever and follow the directions to 'lather, rinse and REPEAT.'

"Never had to send anyone to Red House before now. That's a good ten miles away. Well, what's the address?"

"384 Willie Walker Road." I glanced down the hallway. Granny was nowhere in sight.

"Mercy me," the voice said.

If the lady on the other end of the phone didn't hurry it along, I was going to need a lot of RE-PEATS on Granny's hair to keep her out of mine throughout all of this.

I asked, "Anything else you need?"

"No, but it may be a while. We've only got one officer on duty and he's working the livestock show over in Poca. And you're absolutely sure someone robbed you?"

I thought I heard the back door open. "No, we're the robbers," I whispered as I hung up.

The moment I put down the receiver, I wanted to take it all back. I grabbed the phone and thrust the receiver to my ear but it was too late. The lady was gone and Granny was coming toward me with a huge towel wrapped around the top of her head.

"Winsley-girl, have you seen my reading glasses? Want to read a verse or two in my Bible before service tomorrow. Goodness gracious, that twitch of yours has started up again. Never known anyone to have one last so long or go so fast. You gotta go see someone about it when we get home. It's not becoming for a young lady."

"No to the glasses and yes on going about the twitch. Think I'll turn in now," I answered with a fake yawn.

"Kinda early, isn't it? Did you get all those arithmetic problems solved?"

"No, but I'm tired. I'll finish them later."

"Well, nighty-night then. See you in the morning."

I left Granny hunting for her glasses and Bible. As the full moon rose illuminated the sky, I listened to everyone turn in for the night, and I prayed like

I'd never prayed before. I prayed that someone's prize bull had busted loose and was running willy-nilly and it'd take the policeman half the night to round it up. That way, he'd be too tired to come see about us.

I prayed that if the police did show up, everyone would be asleep and I could talk my way out of it – or hide.

I mean, who in their right mind would send their brother and grandfather to jail? What was I thinking? I was supposed to be watching out for Billy, not sending him to the pokey.

Sometime in the dark of night, the loud snoring across the hall came to a halt and I heard Granny say, "Where ya going?"

"Little Egypt."

"Don't forget to take some paper with you, I'm not bringing it all the way out there in the dark," Granny answered.

I peered through my open window in time to see the back flap of Gramps's long-johns waving in the wind as he darted toward the outhouse. As luck would have it, a car rounded the bend and its bright lights lit up Gramps's behind. Never one to miss an opportunity, Gramps did a little jig.

The car slowed down.

I wanted to die. Just die. Gramps was fixin' to get arrested. And it'd be my fault.

But then I knew the Lord was on my side. I don't

know why he was because a miracle happened. The car picked up speed and sped out of sight.

Now, as Gramps danced his way on down to the privy, I wanted to live. I wanted to jump. I wanted to shout. It wasn't the police. No one was coming out here this late. *Glory, Glory, Hallelujah!* Or if it was the police, Gramps had scared him off. Either way, *Hallelujah, Hallelujah, Halle-le-lu-jah!*

Thank goodness it was all over. No one would ever know what I'd done. I could go home again and Mother wouldn't have to kill me.

Then . . . I heard the ever so faint sound of a distant car motor.

Dim headlights steadily grew brighter.

Go on by, go on by, pleasssse . . . go on by.

DRATS!!

Stay in "Little Egypt!" Stay in "Little Egypt!" PLEASSSSE, Gramps, stay in "Little Egypt!"

DRATS!!

As Gramps made his exodus out of *Little Egypt*, I broke out in a heavy sweat.

Before the squad car had a chance to climb up the driveway and come to a stop, Gramps was walking alongside the driver's window, his hand resting on the roof of the car.

The policeman cut the motor and rolled down his window.

Gramps fanned his hand back-and-forth under his nose. "OOO-EEE . . . You hauling manure?"

"Hey Old-timer, if you're implying that I'm a pig, I'm gonna haul your hiney in. Understand?"

"No disrespect meant, but honest-to-goodness man . . . you smell like um . . . um . . . fertilizer and that ain't no lie."

"I may smell, but here you are with your scrawny old hiney hanging out of your clothes. I ought to lock you up for indecent exposure! And not that it's any of your business, I've been working over at the livestock show and I may have stepped in a pile or two. Now, it's late and I'm tired. But here I am. So, what's the problem?"

"I don't know what you're talking about, fella. I think you've got the wrong place."

"Don't you dare mess with me! An emergency call came in from this house and I'm fixin' to get to the bottom of it."

Gramps might as well been standing next to me when he answered, "You don't say."

I nearly wet my pants.

"Yes, I DO say. Someone at this address phoned in a robbery. In fact, we've had a string of robbery calls from this area in the last couple of days. The Widow Peabody forgot to pull her lawnmower into her shed before dark and when she did, she nearly wound up in the hospital from plopping down where the seat used to be. Worse, over at the cemetery, the cart they use to move caskets from the hearse to gravesites is missing three tires. Now, I might understand someone swiping all four tires, but three

. . . sure seems strange. And you want to know what's even worse?"

"What?" Gramps asked.

"Tomorrow is Myrtle Phiffle's funeral and it's gonna take every man in the county to get her from the car to the grave. She musta weighed well over three hundred pounds."

"You don't say," Gramps repeated.

"Well, anyway . . . what got stolen here?"

"Nothing. Someone in your office must have gotten the numbers mixed-up."

"Not likely," the policeman answered.

Gramps glanced toward my window. "Hmm . . . well . . . the only thing that happened here today was my granddaughter got thrown down a well."

A shiver of cold went through my body.

The policeman let out a long whistle before answering, "Oh, my gaw-sh. What in the name of tarnation happened?"

"Accident, but she climbed back out."

"Want me to run that granddaughter of yours over to Charleston General – just to be on the safe side."

"Nah, she'll live."

Yeah. I get to live!

Gramps nodded. "Kids often bounce back. Of course, sometimes not."

Now I wasn't sure if I was going to get to live or not.

Gramps removed his hand from the roof of the

car. "Sure do appreciate you coming all this way. Well, it's late. Thanks, again."

The policeman didn't say anything for several long minutes.

"Well, if you're sure she's okay, I'll be headin' on. Been a long day and I've still got to stop over at Willie Walker's place. Say, isn't Willie your cousin?"

"That he is. What's the problem over there?" Gramps asked as he leaned closer to the policeman's window.

"Nothing major. He's upset someone's been stealing his good apples for the past several weekends."

Good grief! Who'd think that old man would care! Oh, my gosh! I'd called the police on myself! Great, just great.

"Hardly seems like something the police need to be involved in," Gramps said with another glance toward my window.

The policeman turned the ignition key and his motor purred. "Not that it's any of your business, this time the culprits stole 'em from his best cobbler tree."

"Still . . . hardly seems like something that needs to be reported."

"Reckon I'll be the judge of that."

"Reckon so. Well, off you go," Gramps answered as he slapped the roof of the car.

The policeman gave a short nod as he backed his cruiser down Gramps's grass-worn driveway.

Gramps entered the house and walked down the

hallway, pausing outside my bedroom door for a couple of seconds before moving on to his own.

I didn't sleep much that night. And when I did, I dreamed of Isaac Newton, falling apples and squealing pigs.

The next morning at breakfast, Granny made a point of looking straight at me when she said "Prank calls are against the law, you know."

I didn't answer as I buttered the pitifully small pancake on my plate.

After I poured syrup all over it, Billy handed me a plate of crispy fried bacon and whispered, "This comes from one of those you know . . . you know . . . one of those animals that *squeal*."

Great! They all knew . . . well, so what! Gramps hadn't said a word so he seemed like he was going to let me live, and for the moment, that mattered more than Granny flipping the smallest pancake on my plate.

Chapter 10

~ THE Turquoise T-Bird ~

~ Worry #11 ~

It would take an army

to keep up with Gramps.

I'm not an army.

Monday morning, as Granny and I were shucking ears of corn we'd brought home from the farm, the phone rang. Granny answered and I scooted close to listen. It was Gramps.

"I'm sending Morse Withers for the checkbook."

"Where are you? Thought you'd gone for milk and celery," Granny answered.

What sounded something like "nah, I'm over at Rod's" tinged through the receiver.

Granny's face lit up. She turned to me and said, "Gramps is over at Rod's Car Lot. Imagine that!"

After Granny hung up, we both giggled and then shucked corn like there was no tomorrow. A new car will make a body do that.

Morse Withers was the only taxi that came this far out of Charleston. It was common knowledge Morse was really using his station wagon as a means to stay away from his shrill wife and whiny passel of boys, more than a way to tote people around.

Gramps, on the other hand, said Morse was a genius in our midst, earning a buck or two, all the while tootling around town, listening to music on the radio.

At any rate, Granny could hardly contain her excitement about the prospect of a new car.

Less than a month ago, she had fallen in love with a dark green Cadillac sitting on the lot at Rod's.

"I tell you, that Cadillac is beau-ti-f-o-o-l. I can almost smell that leather just thinkin' about it," Granny said as she waltzed to the trash with two fistfuls of husks.

If anything, I was even more excited than Granny. The way I saw it, a new car was just the trick to make a person forget about building an airplane, especially one that was still in a hundred pieces all over the driveway.

After Morse came for the checkbook, Granny and I worked as fast as we could. Still, it seemed like forever before Granny screwed the lid on the last Mason jar of canned corn. As the jars cooled, we made our way to the front porch.

There, we kept our eyes peeled on the road for the longest time. Eventually, I had to go home to help Mother fix supper.

After dinner, Mother, Billy and I drifted back to keep Granny company as we watched for the shiny dark green Cadillac to glide up.

If you've ever had something turn out the exact opposite of what you pictured, you can imagine the feeling we all had when a turquoise and chrome Thunderbird zoomed up the driveway and skidded to a stop smack in front of us.

I didn't know cars came in colors like that. Gramps always said the acid pollution of nearby chemical plants ate the paint off cars faster than you could spit, and that was why most of the cars in Cross Lanes ended up the same shade of dingy gray. I don't know if that's true, but I do know that a turquoise Thunderbird wasn't like any car I'd ever seen.

Mother let out a gasp. Billy darted toward the car. Granny pulled a small flask out of the pocket of her housedress and poured a good amount of goldeny-brown liquid straight down her throat. After that, she turned and stomped back inside, letting the screen door slam shut behind her.

Gramps rolled down his car window and yelled, "Who wants to go for a spin?"

Mother lied, "Can't. Gotta casserole in the oven."

Gramps should have known a turquoise Thunderbird wasn't the kind of car Mother would be riding in now – or ever.

I walked slowly toward the car.

Gramps passed me going the other way as he bounded toward the house.

I climbed in the car, feeling little and a bit scared surrounded by all of that bright turquoise.

And then we waited . . . and waited, hoping Granny would show her face and we could head down the road.

To hurry things along, Billy tooted the horn every couple of minutes or so.

Nothing.

Eventually, Billy climbed out and ran off.

Since it seemed rude for everyone to leave, I stayed.

Finally, Gramps reappeared. No Granny. Without saying a word, the two of us headed toward the Dairy Queen. As soon as the car came to a complete stop, a crowd gathered around us. Judging from people's comments, I'm not sure everyone thought Gramps's turquoise car was as great as he did.

Dimples's mother was among the lookers. She stated rather loudly, "A little too showy for Cross Lanes, don't you think?"

I thought so, too, and was glad when Gramps spun gravel and we peeled out.

I was pretty sure Dimples would add a turquoise car to the list of things to hold against me. *Great, the list just keeps on growing.*

During the following months whenever the color of the car was mentioned, Gramps would snap, "Ah, who wants to be ordinary?"

To which, Granny never failed to reply, "I do!"

The car stayed, but Granny's trips around Cross Lanes were few and far between.

Any time the car was brought up in Mother's presence, she always said, "Less is best."

When times got tough, Granny and Mother stuck together and a turquoise car is a "tough time" in a small town.

As for me, the trip to the Dairy Queen turned out to be worth the ride. Two business cards were sticking out of Gramps' checkbook in the front seat, one for a welder and another with the phone number of a professor over at the Vocational School in Charleston. I swiped them both.

If Gramps was going to build *Emerald Eyes*, there'd be no help from me – or anyone else, if I could help it. Besides, swiping those business cards was my way of paying Gramps back for not getting Granny the Cadillac. She deserved better than a strange-colored car, even if it was a sporty T-Bird that seemed to float above pot holes in our West Virginia roads.

Chapter 11

~ THE Moral of DUH ~

~ Worry #12 ~

MOTHER is HEadin' FOR THE

LooneY Bin,

SuRE shootin' and Fast!

The new school year was just around the corner, so I wasn't surprised when Dimples called me one evening to say she'd heard sixth grade was a lot of fun.

The two of us agreed there was definitely a feeling of excitement in the air. It would be a new beginning – not that I needed one, not really. The behavior side of my report card always had pluses for "effort" in every single category and my grades were never lower than a "B".

Still, it was a real sore spot with me that Billy, even though his behavior stunk, was a straight "A" student. Didn't seem fair.

Mother and I discussed it every now and then, and usually she gave good advice, but one particular conversation baffled me.

"Winsley, when I was your age, I went to school with a boy named Donnie Meadows. Even though he was always doing things he shouldn't, everything seemed to turn out alright for him."

"What do you mean exactly?" I asked.

"Well . . . for instance, one day at school he pulled the fire alarm as a prank. Fortunately for him, about the same time a rag caught on fire in the chemistry lab. In the end, he was touted as a hero and awarded a Fire Prevention certificate."

"Sounds a lot like Billy," I answered.

"Precisely," Mother replied.

"What became of Donnie Meadows?"

"That's the sad part, Winsley. No one seems to

know. I've often watched Billy and wish't I knew what became of Donnie."

"Probably everything went well for Donnie Meadows, just like it will for Billy."

"Whatever makes you say that?"

I didn't bother to answer Mother and she didn't question me further.

I didn't really understand the point of Mother's story. To me, it meant some people are the "golden ones." Either you are or you aren't. Sadly, I wasn't.

A couple of days later, Mother said, "Winsley, I need to make a quick trip to Franny's to finish up your clothes for school. Wanna go?"

Since I didn't want to show up for sixth grade wearing gnomes or big polka-dots, I decided to tag along. Besides, Mother had been going through ric-rac lickety-split and I planned to thwart the buying of any more – if possible.

As it turned out, Mother's run to Franny's only involved thread and hemming tape, and I was all smiles at the checkout counter until Franny remarked, "Oh, by the way, tell Seth the green Dacron he'd ordered came in."

"Now, why in the world would that grandfather of yours be ordering fabric?" Mother questioned as we went out the door,

"More than likely, to stretch over the frame of *Emerald Eyes*," I sobbed out.

"You mean to tell me that plane is going to be made out of fabric from Franny's? Well, I swanee."

Tears started to roll down my face. "Probably not the *entire* thing . . . but you can bet the WINGS will. How safe could that be?"

"Honestly, Winsley, he's not going to get that far with it. Wipe your eyes and quit worrying."

Quit worrying . . . yeah . . . right.

I tried to ignore the flutter of butterflies in my stomach as I continued to plead with Mother to take matters into her hand. "Mother, don't you see what's happening?"

"Surely you're not worried about all that rusted old junk on the driveway, are you?"

"Yes, I'm worried. Why wouldn't I be? I mean the Dacron, the plane . . . EVERYTHING!"

"Winsley, Seth can gather up all of the stuff he wants, but makin' it fly is a whole 'nuther matter."

I wanted to scream. I wanted to shout that more than likely Donnie Meadows was living the good life in the south of France and Gramps was sky-bound sooner than you'd think.

Chapter 12

~ Miss Dee LaPierre Loves Purple ~

~ Worry #13 ~

We're gonna need more smarts than we've got.
It's as simple as that.

As much as I hated to admit it to anyone other than Dimples, it felt good to be back in school. And it felt REALLY good to be a sixth grader.

Miss Dee LaPierre, our math teacher, was new to the area, and she was beautiful. Very elegant, very glamorous. She'd been to France – not once, but twice! Even though she sprinkled French words throughout every conversation, it was easy to understand what she meant. Best of all, she was the exact opposite of Hinkle. Hinkle was one of us – country folk. Miss Dee LaPierre was definitely not.

As Dimples and I walked home from school on the first day, I remarked, "Dimples, isn't Miss Dee LaPierre simply divine? I love the way she wears her black hair in a French twist. She looks like a movie star – a French Movie Star."

Never one to be impressed easily, Dimples answered, "Um . . . I guess."

"Sure she does. Hinkle couldn't get her frizzy gray hair to look like that, if her life depended on it."

Dimples burst out laughing. "Well, then, it's a good thing it doesn't."

"Did you notice how Miss Dee LaPierre writes everything in purple? I mean, who doesn't love purple? I bet Mr. Grayson could order some purple ink pens for the rest of us, don't you?"

Dimples seemed to be thinking it over before replying. "You know how he is. He probably wouldn't do it if we asked, just for spite. And anyway, Miss Dee LaPierre may be more glamorous than Miss Hinkle but Miss Hinkle will be always thought of as "the fish that got away."

"The fish that got away? What are you talking about?"

"Well, when I took my inhaler to the clinic today, I heard some gossip, that's what."

"What kind of gossip?"

Dimples looked back toward the school before leaning closer and whispering, *"Teacher Gossip."*

"Teacher gossip?" I stopped walking, anxious for Dimples to tell more.

"Yes . . . TEACHER GOSSIP. Teachers do gossip, you know. After all, they're humans, too. They eat, sleep and well, you know."

"Okay, okay, I get it. Teachers are human . . . and they gossip. So, what exactly did you hear?"

"One of the teachers . . . who shall remain nameless . . . said that Edith Hinkle is one lucky fish if she is able to quit teaching and selling *Avon* to go into real estate or move to Myrtle."

"Hinkle's quiting?"

"Now, Winsley, promise me that you won't repeat one word of this. I need that inhaler."

"I'm not promising anything. Besides, I doubt there's anyone in Cross Lanes that doesn't already know Hinkle's quitting — except us kids, of course."

Dimples hurried to catch up with me as I started to cross the street in front of Grayson's.

"Promise me, Winsley, I mean it."

I shifted my backpack before answering. "Don't you think every kid at the elementary school knows by now? I mean, it is the first day of school."

"Yeah, you're right. Still, I don't want my name spread around with the fact that she quit."

"Seems a pity she didn't get out of teaching before embarrassing me half-to-death. And since when do you need an inhaler?"

Dimples laughed. "Actually, I don't. But you have to go through the office to get to the clinic. So, let's just say an inhaler – any inhaler, is a free pass to roam around the office area. And what's more, no one seems to notice that you're there."

"But what if they make you use the inhaler and you don't even need it?"

"There is no "they" in the clinic, just the school nurse. Besides, my inhaler is an old empty one I found, you big Do-Do Bird."

"Sneaky, Dimples . . . and very clever, I must say."

"I thought so, too," she answered with one of her dimply smiles.

We parted ways at the end of Gramps's long driveway and I headed on home alone. The closer I got, the more I wanted to cry.

Among long green strips of Dacron hanging on the porch rail sat several older Cross Lanes boys. Boys I recognized. Boys who spent their days over at the Vocational School in Charleston! I don't know how he did it, but even without the business card, Gramps had somehow pried kids away from their classes and lured them into his yard. Unbelievable!

Worse, there was a plane. A miniature-looking

one – but a plane, nonetheless! Okay . . . to be honest, it was only a bunch of tubing and pipes that kinda formed the outline of one. Still, it looked close enough to the real thing to make me shiver. Smack in the middle of all the confusion stood Gramps. He had grease on his clothes and a grin on his face. When he saw me, he waved me over with a large wrench in his hand.

I took a couple of steps his way and then stopped, wishing I could escape the soon-to-be-disaster that would surely wipe us all from the face of the earth. That is, if and when Gramps got the dang thing to fly.

With a wide grin on his face, Gramps motioned to me again and yelled, "Before you know it, I'll be dodgin' clouds and chasing rainbows. You're gonna love it, Winsley-girl, jest you wait and see."

I didn't trust myself not to burst into tears so I didn't answer.

Never one to wait a second-and-a-half, Gramps said, "Come on over here and giddy-up about it."

I speeded up until I was standing beside him.

Gramps looked down and me and said, "Aw, quit worrying. By the way, that twitch of yours is actin' up bad."

I wanted to tell him that the only way my twitch was likely to take a vacation was if he lit a match to his beloved *Emerald Eyes*. But I kept quiet. He'd be disappointed enough when it sunk in his brain that there wasn't a chance Mother was going to let me or

Billy get within shooting distance of his dang plane once it was finished, much less fly around in it.

I darted inside and slung my backpack on Granny's kitchen table.

Before I had time to think about what I should do, I heard Gramps yelling my name. *Good grief.*

I poked my head out the screen door.

"Did that fancy teacher of yours send me the stuff I asked for?"

"What stuff?"

"Math stuff – calculations, angle of attack and all that stuff."

Angle of attack! What was this crazy grandfather of mine planning? Maybe Hinkle was right. Maybe Gramps was a crackpot – and one that was planning on dropping bombs on all of us good West Virginians! Things were worse than I thought!

Trying to act nonchalant, I shrugged my shoulders.

"Well, did she or didn't she?" Gramps said in a louder voice.

"No. She didn't send a thing."

Not one to give up easily, he answered, "Check your backpack."

I went back to the kitchen and dumped out my backpack. A couple of books hit Granny's table with a dull thud and a couple of pencils rolled to the edge. In the midst of it all, a piece of paper fluttered to the floor. A folded note. You'd think by now anything that involved Gramps would definitely

NOT come as a surprise. As I bent down to pick it up, the sight of all that purple caught me off guard.

After making sure Gramps was not coming inside to check my backpack himself, I unfolded the paper. Mathematical calculations covered it from top-to-bottom. There was a lot math showing how to reduce the scale of regular-sized plane. On the back of the paper was information about ratios, load carrying capacity, range, speed and other airplane stuff. Everything, I mean EVERYTHING, was written in fancy handwriting – PURPLE handwriting. I didn't need to read the signature at the bottom but my eyes went there anyway. Hooked to the "e" at the end of her last name was little purple Eiffle Tower. *Well, LAH-DE-DAH!*

I ripped the Eiffle Tower, her signature, and that purple math into tiny little pieces. I pulled the trash can out from under the sink and stuffed torn-up bits of purple and paper under old coffee grounds and some broken egg shells in the bottom of the trash, before screaming out the screen door, "NO, NOTHING. SHE DIDN'T SEND A THING!"

I figured if you placed "lying" on one side of a balance scale and "dying in a plane crash" on the other side, the two would never balance out to be the same.

Never one to let things go, Gramps yelled back, "Never mind. I'll stop by the school and talk to Mademoiselle LaPierre myself."

Great.

Chapter 13

~ THE TRAVELERS GET READY TO DEPART ~

~ WORRY #14 ~

REMEMBER: It would take an ARMY?
I AM NOT AN ARMY!
WORSE, SOME OF MY MOST
DEPENDABLE SOLDIERS ARE
going AWOL.

Rain.

Hallelujah!

More Rain.

Hallelujah!

Work on the airplane at a standstill.

Voc Tech boys have disappeared.

Hallelujah, Hallelujah, Hal-le-lu-jah!.

Sunshine.

Drats, and drats, and drats again – forever and ever. Amen.

Before muddy puddles had time to dry up, Granny got a phone call from her sister Midge who lived in Poca. Poca was a good twenty minutes down the road – the opposite direction from Charleston. Unfortunately, Midge had tumbled down a ladder and hit her head, all from trying to change a light bulb. Not only that, her leg was broken and she needed Granny's help.

I prayed Granny would demand that Gramps stop where he was on the airplane and go with her, but that hope was lost when she said, "With Midge feeling poorly, I'll be able to better concentrate on helping her without anyone else around. Besides, arriving in that dang turquoise car might be too much for my dear frail sister. I'll call Morse. He can carry me there."

As she pulled her suitcase from the back of her closet, I heard her say to herself, "What's more, I'd rather die than to breeze into Poca looking like the Queen of England."

I prayed Gramps would insist on going with her. But he only handed her his wallet and said, "Take out enough money for Morse, and then some, just in case you need to stay longer."

Morse was called.

Granny left.

If Granny's leaving wasn't enough, Daddy came home from work with a huge grin on his face. "First of next week, they're sending me to Canton, Ohio. Yes, indeed . . . Canton, Ohio. Going for a week-long seminar. And, get this, since my room is paid for, the boss said it'd be okay to take the little wife along."

I ducked my head in case Mother hurled the pot she was washing across the room. She wasn't one to take to the phrase "the little wife." When I looked up, it came as a huge surprise to hear her laughing. "Well, I declare. I never expected to be going any-where – not like this, so out of the blue."

I could not believe what I was hearing.

Mother handed me the pot to finish drying.

I questioned, "But aren't you forgetting some-thing?"

"What's that?" Mother asked.

"Granny's gone to her sister's house."

"Um . . . I'll have to see what I can work out. Could be a problem."

Unable to help myself, I burst out, "COULD be a problem. If you ask me, it IS a problem and not a little one, at that. I know what you can do – not go, that's what."

"Don't be silly, Winsley. We won't be gone that long. You'll be fine. You and Billy will be in school during the day and you can stay with Gramps at night."

"But Mom . . ."

"Listen, I tell you what. I'll ask Dimples's mom to keep an eye on things. How's that?"

"But . . . what about Billy? You know how he is. Aren't you nervous about leaving him? I bet if Dad's boss knew our situation, he'd tell him to bring his kids along, too."

"Now . . . you heard what Dad said – wives only. But if it will make you feel any better, I'll promise Billy to bring him something if he behaves. Quit worrying, sweetie. Things will be fine."

I didn't answer. What was there to say? Apparently, thoughts of a Canton vacation had addled Mother's brain.

I searched my brain for some way to get through to her and tried again, "Don't you think maybe you should stay here and see about Midge? I mean . . . she is Granny's sister and hitting her head can't be a good thing. I know you'd feel really bad if she died and you weren't here for Granny."

"Winsley, I wouldn't say this to another living soul, but that Midge is mean as a snake, always has been. I don't know how she and your Granny could have come from the same family. So, no, I'm not aiming to give up my vacation on account of her."

Great. Now what?

Well, at least, Mother made good on her word to speak to Dimples's mom because on the way to school the next morning, Dimples greeted me with, "Do you honestly think your mom should be going out of town right now?"

"No. Definitely not!"

"Neither do I. In fact, we were all surprised she would even think of leaving home with everything . . . everything . . . uh . . . like it is."

"Me, too. Guess it just goes to show you, grown-ups aren't as smart as everyone thinks they are."

Dimples patted my shoulder. "Some of them are and some of them aren't."

She didn't need to tell me which ones were and which ones weren't. I already knew that.

We continued walking but I barely bothered to listen to what she had to say until she tapped my shoulder. "I mean . . . Canton, . . . of all places. I might understand your Mother losing her head over London or Paris or some place like that, but . . . Canton, Ohio!"

"Me, too," I answered.

Well, if there's anything that I can do, let me know."

"Actually, there may be."

"Anything . . . just say the word."

"Think you're gonna need that inhaler of yours today, Dimples?"

"Well . . . that depends. What do you need?"

"Is there a telephone book in the clinic?"

"Sure is . . . right next to a big case of tissues."

"I'm gonna need the number for the Vocational Tech School, the one over in Charleston?"

"You'll have it by lunch."

I gave Dimples a smile and answered, "See you out front for lunch . . . and thanks."

The morning crept along but eventually the lunch bell sounded.

I made a wild dash for the long brick wall in front of the school. It was the place where kids who brought their lunch congregated.

Dimples arrived minutes later and handed me a slip of paper.

"Thanks, Dimples. I owe you one."

"No problem and good luck." She unwrapped a peanut butter sandwich. "But promise me when this is all over, you'll see someone about that eye. It's getting worse all the time. No one's going to want to date you until you get it taken care of."

"It's not like I'm looking for a boyfriend, but if it will make you feel any better, I promise."

Dimples laughed. "Well, you never know who's looking at you."

"And Dimples, I never told you this, but I'm glad both of your grandfathers live in Kentucky . . . and you've got good Christian brothers."

"Thanks," she answered, "And about the cemetery missing flower-thing . . . your secret is safe with me."

"Ah, you're the best. I knew you must have figured it out by now."

Since there wasn't anything left to say, I took a sip of apple juice from my thermos and opened the wax paper around my peanut butter sandwich. Then, I handed Dimples my chocolate chip cookie. She deserved it. After all, the seven numbers in the palm of my hand were all that stood between me and disaster.

On the way home from school, I stopped at Grayson's. It was the only place in all of Cross Lanes that had a pay phone. The trick would be placing the call when no one was in hearing-distance on my end of the phone.

After scrounging for a couple of coins in the bottom of my backpack, I pretended to tie my shoes when Mr. Grayson walked by me. As soon as he trundled outside to retrieve a grocery cart, I shoved a couple of coins in phone's narrow slot and dialed.

A woman answered. "Good afternoon. Vo-Tech of Charleston. How may I help you?"

"Yes, this is the wife of Seth Walker and he . . . uh . . . he uh . . . asked for some help building an airplane but he . . . uh . . . he uh . . . doesn't need any more help," I stammered, trying to sound older than I was. "So, you can get everyone back to school . . . and you need to do it soon as possible. Okay?"

"Are you sure, Mrs. Walker?"

"Quite. He's changed his mind, but wanted me to thank you just the same."

"Ummm . . . changed his mind. That's funny. He phoned here no more than an hour ago to see if we had a welder we could send out."

Drats!

I took a deep breath. "He changes his mind a lot. And since I'm his wife, I guess I should know."

"You sound awfully young," the voice answered.

"I'm his second wife . . . and quite a bit younger than his first!"

"Humm . . . is that so?"

"Yes and bye now. Remember, NO MORE STUDENTS. And uh . . . Seth sends his thanks just the same."

Wondering if I'd pulled off the impossible, I gave a nervous laugh as I replaced the receiver.

"Glad to hear you're over your terrible loss."

I whirled around to face the delivery man! *Drats!*

I nodded. "I tell you . . . it was a miracle. A miracle! Guess you've heard by now, Gramps didn't die after all. A doctor in Charleston got the chicken bone out. I tell you, we've done nothing but celebrate. In fact, we celebrate morning, noon and night – all of us. That's the exact reason you heard me laughing. We're all downright giddy over his recovery. None of us can stop laughing, no matter where we are, or what we're doing. We laugh all the time."

"Is that so?" the man answered with a raised eyebrow.

I let loose with my very best laugh, picked up my backpack and ran for home, as if my life depended on it.

Chapter 14

~ GRAMPS, BillY and the LEPRECHauns ~

~ WORRY #15 ~

No GRannY.

No MOtHER.

No Dad,

Just GRaMPS, BillY and ME.

'NuFF ZEd!

I guess second wives don't count. In spite of my phone call, students continued to make their way up Gramps's driveway. A second welder, too. They all had tool belts slung over their shoulder with tools that glistened as if they'd never been used.

The more the Voc Tech boys showed up in Gramps's yard that Monday morning, the more I pleaded with Mother to put a stop to it all. Unfortunately, in all the excitement of going somewhere, she'd apparently lost her mind.

As Daddy threw a couple of suitcases in the car, she poured orange juice on her cereal and tucked a spoon behind her ear. Neither Billy nor I said a word, but we held onto our silverware and slurped up our milky cereal.

As Mother and Daddy flew down the driveway, Billy and I trudged toward school.

Later that morning, while Miss Dee LaPierre wrote math problems on the board, I decided if I ever had kids, I'd never go to Canton and I'd better document everything while my irresponsible parents were frolicking in Ohio. That way, if things at home turned ugly or we ended up in the pokey, I'd have a detailed account of it all.

After turning in my seatwork, I drew some little dancing leprechauns on the front of my worry spiral and made a paper pocket to hold all future plane documentation I was likely to accumulate.

I decided not to show my notes to anyone unless a catastrophe occurred. Of course, I used my best

117

handwriting, knowing there was a chance Chief Knight, or maybe even the Air Force, would be poring over my every word.

When I came home from school that day, I shielded my eyes from seeing what the Voc Tech boys had done that day.

Later that evening, as I was brushing my teeth, Gramps stopped in the bathroom doorway and said, "Your Granny called. She's enjoying her little vacation. She's not plannin' on coming home for several more days."

I couldn't think of an answer to that so I just spit in the sink. I guess Gramps didn't expect an answer because when I looked back to the doorway, he'd moved on down the hall toward his own bed.

Back in Granny's guestroom, I flipped open my spiral notebook and wrote the following:

Day: Monday
Time: 800 hours (8 in the morning)
Event: Parents Left

Day: Same Monday
Time: 1600 hours (4:00 in the afternoon)
Event: Frame of plane finished. Looks really little. We Walkers are skinny, but we're not midgets. We might be too big to fit!

Day: Same Monday
Time: 1800 hours (6:00 in the evening)
Event: Gramps ate bread and butter. Forgot about Billy and me.

Day: Same Monday
Time: 1900 hours (7:00 in the evening)
Event: Billy and me each ate a jar of Granny's canned corn - cold.

Day: Same Monday
Time: 2000 hours (8:00 in the evening)
Event: My stomach hurts - bad.

Tuesday, I hurried through my work at school and spent my study hall time in the library looking for airplane books, all the while dreading what I'd find when I got home from school. Since the plane was so tiny, there was always the chance it'd be finished.

As I walked up the hill that afternoon, I saw a little green mosquito. Of course, the closer I got, the bigger it grew. And by the time I reached Gramps's driveway, that itty mosquito turned into a plane with bright green canvas stretched from the tip of one wing to the tip of the other. In sparkly gold paint, the words "Emerald-Eyed Baby" glistened across its belly. My lip trembled and I wanted to cry at the sight of that mean little death machine.

Cute? Yes. Deadly? Yes. My worst fears had come true, nail-by-nail and screw-by-screw.

When Gramps greeted me with "Bonjour Mademoiselle," I knew he'd talked with Miss Dee LaPierre. She was the only person in all of Cross Lanes that would have a person spouting French like that. Sure enough, in his hand was a sheet of lavender paper covered with purple calculations from top to bottom. And in the bottom corner was Miss Dee LaPierre's purple signature along with a little hand-sketched Eiffle Tower.

Feeling sick, I dropped my backpack on Granny's front porch and sat down to watch the Voc Tech guys. Scurrying from the plane to Gramps's garage, they looked like ants at a picnic.

I wanted to run away from the sight of the plane, Gramps, and the Voc Tech boys but I was stuck like glue. My feet wouldn't move. Billy followed whatever Voc Tech boy didn't shoo him away.

After an eternity, work stopped and the Voc Tech boys disappeared, one-by-one.

Even though the sun had set, the house felt stuffy when I entered. I open my backpack and pulled out my spiral. As I wrote, I wondered who would be the first to read my words. After careful consideration, I dismissed Chief Knight and the Air Force, figuring in times of crisis, they probably sent the Army.

Well, too late, Army. Too late. Where were you when I needed you!

At the end of the day, my notes looked like this:

Day: Tuesday
Time: 1630 hours (4:30 in the afternoon)
Event: Granny phoned. Not ready to come home.
Who can blame her?

Day: Same Tuesday
Time: 1700 hours (5:00 in the evening)
Event: Plane now has wires, gears and a lot of
other stuff.

Day: Same Tuesday
Time: 1730 hours (5:30 in the afternoon)
Event: Billy hitched a ride to the Dairy Queen. I
stayed home to keep an eye on Gramps.

Day: Same Tuesday
Time: 1830 hours (6:30 in the evening)
Event: I got a half-eaten French fry in the bottom of Billy's bag, along with a cold hot dog. I
didn't even care there was a bite missing in the
middle of the hot dog. At least Billy made it back
home - alive.

Day: Same Tuesday
Time: 2000 hours (8 in the evening)
Event: My stomach hurts worse than yesterday.

Later that same night, as I was drifting off to sleep, the phone in Granny's kitchen rang.

I'd left Gramps at the kitchen table scraping rust from the top of some old spark plugs when I went to bed, so I knew he was in easy reach of the phone.

Gramps's voice boomed when he answered the phone. "Hello."

I crept down the hall to listen.

"Muffle," sounded the voice on the other line.

"We're fine ... no reason to hurry back," Gramps said.

"Muffle, muffle."

Billy now stood huddled beside me.

Neither of us said a word.

Gramps cleared his throat. "We're fine. Stay. Stay as long as you want. Be a dang shame to be that close to the Football Hall of Fame and not see it."

Oh, my gosh! Since when do my parents care a hoot about football?

"Muffle, muffle, muffle."

"Well, alrighty then. We'll see the two of you on Saturday. Bye-bye now."

The receiver made a clanking noise as Gramps dropped it down in its cradle.

Billy looked up at me with a wide grin on his face.

I threw up my hands, wondering what kind of parents would abandon their kids during this critical time. *Canton must be a dang hootenanny or they'd done lost their minds.*

Without turning toward us, Gramps cleared his throat. "Your parents are staying over. Doing some sightseein'. Won't be back until the weekend. Now, get to sleep. Tomorrow is a big day."

Billy danced in his socks back to his cot in Granny's sewing room.

I shuffled back to Granny's guestroom, holding my stomach.

I heard Gramps wind the mantle clock in the living room.

I tiptoed to the medicine cabinet in the hall bathroom and scrounged around for anything that might shoo my butterflies away. No such luck.

The sound of Gramps's boots dropping on the wooden floor in his bedroom was my clue to make my way back to the kitchen to fix some chocolate milk to help me sleep.

Unfortunately, the milk carton sat empty on the counter and there was no cocoa to be found. Not only did my stomach hurt, now the room was spinning. What in the name of tarnation were my parents thinking? Had they completely lost their minds?

I finally gave up on finding anything to calm my stomach or help me sleep, but anyway . . . I needed time to think.

Back in Granny's guest bedroom, I fluffed my pillow and sat up in bed. Besides, there'd be time to sleep later – if we lived through everything.

Tomorrow is a big day. We'll see. If Gramps

wants to kill himself, fine. There's nothing I can do about it. But Billy . . . I'm going to keep that kid alive, or die trying, until those parents of ours decide to sashay home. Of course, Billy will want to play hooky to go up in the plane and Gramps is just the person to let him do it. Well, those two have another thing coming. Billy is goin' to school with me if I have to carry him all the way there . . . and back!

I grabbed my spiral, the one with the leprechauns.

Day: Still Tuesday
Time: 2130 hours (9:30 in the evening)
Event: Gramps said "Tomorrow is a big day" so I've got to find a way to stop the plane.

After reading what I'd written, I tucked my pencil in the spiral and dropped everything to the floor.

That night, I dreamed leprechauns hijacked an airplane bound for Canton. Mother and Daddy were on board. They were eating peanuts, drinking cokes, and laughing. They didn't even seem to care when Chief Knight stood up and announced "Seth Walker, your fans want you to take a bow." At that exact moment, the plane hit some turbulence, causing the pilot's door to fly open. There, in the captain's seat, sat Gramps! As he turned and waved, I awoke in a cold sweat, hating both leprechauns . . . and Ohio.

Chapter 15

~ THE Angle of Attack ~

~ Worry #16 ~

IF the airplane-thing
Keeps Happening,
I'm going to beat Mother
To the Looney Bin!

I grabbed Billy's hand after breakfast the next morning and didn't let go until he disappeared through the double doors of the elementary school.

After making a dash next door to my middle school, time crept along as my teachers droned on.

Finally, the lunch bell sounded. Dimples beat me to the stone wall outside. I shimmied up and whispered in her ear, "I'm gonna pull out all the spark plugs when I get home."

"Won't your grandfather see you? He's always out there."

"I'll wait until he goes to the garage to hunt for a tool or something."

"Good luck," Dimples replied.

I twisted the top off of my thermos and took a sip of milk before dropping some heavy-duty airplane jargon on her. "And oh, just so you'll know, a plane's *Angle of Attack* is the angle between the nose of the aircraft and its velocity vector."

Dimples stopped unwrapping her sandwich. "The what?"

I twisted the top of my thermos open before answering. "The velocity vector."

"The velocity what?"

"Oh, never mind," I answered, as I dug in my pocket for a folded piece of paper.

I took a bite out of my peanut butter and jelly sandwich before saying, "And if removing the spark plugs doesn't work, then look at this."

I handed Dimples the paper and she began to read.

Winsley Walker's
Ways to Stop A Plane

Plan A

Unbolt Engine From wooden block,
So when the Engine begins to
shiver and shake, out it Falls.

Plan B

Cut ignition wires.

Plan C

PRY out starter switch.

Dimples handed the list back to me. Where'd you learn all this stuff?

"From books," I answered.

"What books?"

"Remember our nonfiction section?"

"The one from the Bookmobile?"

"I didn't lug those heavy books home for nothing," I answered with a laugh.

I took another bite of my sandwich as Dimples folded the paper and handed it back to me.

I thrust the note in my pocket and reached for my thermo again. "Doubt I'd be able to twist the bolts hard enough to get the engine loose, but I figure I could easily snip the plane's ignition wires. Unfortunately, Gramps would be able to fix them in no time. A little rewiring and it'd be ready to go. Umm . . . guess I'll go with the starter switch. What do you think?"

"I think you're gonna need a Plan D."

"Plan D?" I asked.

"If Hinkle knows anything about the plane, you're gonna need another plan." Dimples pointed toward a tall figure leaving the elementary school and heading our way.

Hinkle! *Drats!*

"What's she doing here? Shouldn't she be teaching, or off selling *Avon* . . . or real estate . . . or something."

"Well, she's here now. And Winsley, it looks like she heading straight for you."

Great!

Of course Hinkle, being Hinkle, let loose, spitting all over me.

After her embarrassing outburst about my "crackpot grandfather" and the fact that "all of Cross Lanes was laughing their heads off," I knew I would not, could not, stand by and watch Gramps fail in front of the whole wide world. My efforts to sabotage his little green mosquito airplane were playing right into Hinkle's hands, all of Cross Lanes', too. And now, to have even a glimmer of hope to turn things around, I'd have to work like the dickens in order to increase Gramps's odds of getting his beloved *Emerald Eyes* off the ground. *Drats.* It was going to be hard to flip the switch in my brain, but there was no getting out of it. It had to be done – even if we fell from the sky! If Hinkle had anything to do with it, we were goners either way.

Hinkle said Gramps was a crackpot. Well, so what? We all are. It runs in the family. There's no crime in that. We haven't hurt or maimed anyone . . . yet. *What is that lady's problem?*

Gramps was old. Everyone knows old people don't think straight. He'd lived a lot of years. Seems like that would be worth celebrating. *Guess not.*

What if, by some chance, Gramps proved everyone wrong? What harm could there be in flying around in an itty-bitty plane? Who would we be hurting? Besides, if we killed ourselves, then we'd only have ourselves to blame. Of course, someone would have to say a few words over our graves, but other than that, what harm could we do? The whole lot of us were small people. So, even if we fell from the sky and landed on someone, we might not even flatten them.

The peanut butter and jelly got lodged in my throat while I was trying to nod and shake my answers to Hinkle. I reached for my thermos as Hinkle's tsks floated away and took the cup of chocolate pudding Dimples offered me.

Chapter 16

~ Mosquitoes that Hop ~

(AFTER Hinkle's Hissie-Fit)

~ Worry #17 ~

WE'RE still a long waY FROM
WHERE WE need to be, And it's
not looking good THAT WE'RE
EVER going to get THERE.

As soon as school was out for the day, I slung my backpack on my shoulder and ran home.

My worst fears were confirmed when I spotted Gramps in the pilot's seat of *Emerald Eyes*. The plane was rolling across the yard in the weirdest way. The little plane, not much longer than a Volkswagen Beetle, was actually hopping and skipping across the yard. Every so often, it seemed to jump into the air and fly for several seconds before touching back down again. The whole thing looked like a giant grasshopper. As worried as I felt inside, I wanted to laugh. I could only imagine what all of Cross Lanes would have to say.

I dropped my backpack on the grass and ran behind the plane, trying to get close enough to hear what Gramps was yelling. It was no use. The motor drowned out everything.

After a couple of laps around the yard, Gramps cut the motor, climbed out and said to no one in particular, "Still got a few kinks to work out."

I tugged on his shirt sleeve. "Maybe you've got a kink in the fuel line."

"Why, Winnie-girl, that's some good thinkin'. What in the world made you think of that?"

"I don't know," I answered.

"I always figured that smart brain of yours would come in handy one day."

Spurred on by Hinkle's words, I smiled at Gramps. "I bet if we try, we can solve *Emerald Eyes's* problem – together."

Gramps smiled back. "Sounds like a plan to me."

"Well . . . we know we're getting enough fuel SOME of the time because *Emerald Eyes* does go up. Maybe she doesn't stay there because there's not enough gasoline flowing through the fuel line *all* of the time."

"I declare, I can't believe I didn't think of that."

I cautioned, "Don't get too excited . . . until we know for sure."

"Gotcha," Gramps answered.

"Well, at least it's worth a shot. Are you sure you've got gasoline in both tanks?"

Gramps took a bandana out of his back pocket and wiped his forehead. "Yes, indeed, filled 'em last night."

"Okay . . . then we know it's something else. Maybe something to do with the propulsion system. I don't know, but . . . seeing as how some of the tubes you used were a bit rusted and dented, I'm betting . . . you've got a kink in the line somewhere that's keeping the gasoline from flowing at a steady rate."

"Propulsion system? Where did you learn about that?"

"In one of Mr. Farley's books."

Gramps laughed. "Well, I'll be. Winnie-girl, you may very well be the answer to my prayers."

"Don't thank me yet . . . not until we know for sure."

"Well, what are we waiting for? Let's check it out. I'm going to hoist this baby back up on blocks and take another look. And I do believe there's a twenty-dollar bill in my pocket with your name on it, if'n you're right."

I smiled and prayed that:

    a. It was a kink in the line, an easy fix.
    b. He'd fly once and that would be the
        end of that.
    c. Hinkle would feel bad about her outburst.
    d. Those on the ground or in the air
        would live to tell about it.

I said a quick prayer and "crossed my heart 'n hoped to fly" over the whole situation and grabbed a sheet of plywood from a stack leaning against the Gramps's garage.

I watched Gramps rock three concrete blocks down in the ground a couple of inches. As soon as he proclaimed they were as steady as they were ever likely to be, I dragged the plywood to him and went back for two more sheets.

Together, we made three ramps, one for each tire of the plane. Then, the two of us lugged, pushed and pulled the plane until that little grasshopper rolled up the planks.

"Winnie-girl, slide on under there and take a look. See if you can spot a kink in any of the pipes or tubing," Gramps said as soon as he put a stick under one of the front tires.

I went down on my knees and then flipped over to my back. Using my heels, I shoved my body under the plane. As I ran my hand along every piece of tubing, I couldn't help but think maybe it was good thing we were a skinny bunch after all. A fat person couldn't have done what I'd just accomplished.

After I slid out, I told Gramps, "Couldn't find a kink – not one. But some of the parts are a bit rusted in places. Still . . . no holes. Other than that, everything seems okay."

Gramps threw down the bandana he had been wiping his face with and said, "Wouldn't you know it! Now what?"

I wanted to say that maybe now was the time to forget the whole thing. And I probably would have too, if Hinkle's words weren't still zooming around in my brain.

I looked Gramps dead-on and answered, "Now, we try to find what's wrong and fix it. That's what."

"Of course, you're right. This here emerald-eyed baby was meant to fly," he answered with a laugh and a pat to the plane's side.

Even though I was committed to helping Gramps get his plane in the air, I needed time to think it through. Maybe Hinkle knew what she was talking about. Maybe none of us had the brains to pull this off without killing ourselves, or someone else.

In order to stall for time while I got my thoughts together, I remarked, "Gramps, we've got to figure out something for dinner. Billy and me, we've been mighty hungry for the past couple of days."

"Speakin' of that brother of yours, where is he?"

"Don't know, and to tell you the truth, that's been bothering me."

"Don't fret. I 'spect he'll show up directly," Gramps answered. "And just where are those Voc Tech boys?"

"I don't know. Maybe they're taking finals or something this week. Who knows," I answered, wishing I hadn't made that phone call. We needed those guys after all. *Drats!*

"And Gramps . . . about that twenty with my name on it, how's 'bout me goin' to Grayson's for something to make for dinner?"

"Good idea. In the meantime, I've got some investigating to do."

Gramps handed me a twenty before ducking his head into the plane's cockpit.

I knew it wasn't likely that he'd find the answer to his problem there, but I kept quiet. My steps were slow as I walked down the hillside toward Grayson's.

Once inside the store, I searched the aisles for something I could fix by myself. After pulling a box of mac and cheese off of the top shelf, I slung a loaf of bread in my cart and headed to the deli for some sliced turkey.

For some unknown reason, Mr. Grayson was in a talkative mood as he wrapped several slices of turkey for me. "This here turkey is what they're calling 'low carb'."

I didn't really care what kind of turkey we ate but I nodded to be polite. "Never heard of that before. What's that mean?"

"Let's just say that it's good for you," he answered, handing me a slim package in white butcher paper.

"Thanks, Mr. Grayson."

I followed him to the cash register.

As Mr. Grayson rang up my items, I knew the answer to Gramps's airplane problem. Carbs . . . CARBURATOR!

Now, if I could only remember what I read about making adjustments on one. *Drats!* I should have swiped that book from Farley. I could have turned in *Jo's Boys* as the twelfth book and he never would have known I still had the plane book, the one about making repairs. Of course, I would have known and it would have bothered me every minute of the day for the rest of my life – or until I turned all books in, of course.

Back at Gramps's, we gobbled down the macaroni and cheese along with a turkey sandwich. Afterwards, in my spiral notebook, I wrote the following:

Day: Thursday
Time: 1500 hours (3:00 in the afternoon)
Event: Little Grasshopper (AKA: Emerald Eyes) not ready to fly.

Day: Same Thursday
Time: 1700 hours (5:00 in the afternoon)
Event: Billy turned up in time for Mac & Cheese and a Turkey Sandwich

Chapter 17

~ Disaster Strikes ~

~ Worry #18 ~

Reading about something

is not the same

as doing it!

At school the next day, things rolled along as usual until math class. As soon as we all got seated and Miss Dee LaPierre told us to get out our books, I tore a sheet out of my worry spiral and wrote a note to Dimples.

Do You REMEMbER anYtHing about caRbuREtoRs FROM tHE books in ouR nonFiction sEction?

When Miss Dee LaPierre turned to write an equation on the board, I folded my note and tapped the shoulder of the kid seated in front of me. I handed him the note and motioned for him to pass it to Dimples.

I watched Dimples unfold the note and then shove it in the back of her math book without making the slightest effort to answer it, or even turn around and nod my way.

Guess I'm on my own. If only I could remember.

Since Miss Dee LaPierre had taken to wearing purple nail polish and using lavender chalk on the board, it seemed like Dimples, and everyone else, was in a trance.

As Miss Dee LaPierre wrote, purple chalk dust filled the air.

In the middle of all that purple, the door opened and shiny cowboy boots clicked across the linoleum floor. A man swaggered in like he owned the place. In a second, the way his large ring of keys rattled when he walked gave him away. His run-down old tennis shoes were gone and he'd traded in his usual wrinkled work shirt for a neatly pressed one. *English Leather* filled the air along with Clayton Peavy, our school janitor, instead of his usual scent: Pinesol.

I watched Peavy. He watched Miss Dee La-Pierre as he screwed a shiny new pencil sharpener to the wall.

The classroom windows were open and a gentle breeze ruffled the notebook paper on my desk. Even though I should have been paying attention to Miss Dee LaPierre, I couldn't take my eyes away from Peavy and the pencil sharpener. As he turned a screwdriver, the twist of his wrist brought an image of an engine to my mind. A sketch of a fan turning in front of an engine from one of the airplane books I'd checked out from the Bookmobile flashed in front of my eyes.

Peavy turned the screwdriver as I watched the propeller jump to life.

Gasoline needs both fuel and air in order to burn. (Page 112)

Another turn of the screwdriver.

Too little fuel, sputter and spurt. (Page 113)

Twist and turn.

Too much air, mixture too rich. (Page 114)

With the last and final twist of Peavy's wrist, our shiny new pencil sharpener was secure. Did he impress Miss Dee LaPierre? I doubted it . . . but maybe.

Not too little, not too much – a simple fix. (Page 115)

As soon as class was over, I elbowed my way through clumps of pokey-walking classmates and sprinted to catch up with Dimples as she neared the stone wall. Once seated, we both yanked the wax paper away from our sandwiches.

After trading my peanut butter for her ham and cheese, I said, "Hey Dimples, guess what?"

"Vhat?" she answered, her mouth full of peanut butter.

"Remember our nonfiction section last summer? You know . . . the books we checked out from the Bookmobile?"

"Of course, I do. They were boring. Give me a good Nancy Drew and I'm happy."

"I know, but just you wait and see, the time I spent reading the nonfiction ones is going to come in handy," I answered, trying not to giggle.

"How's that?"

"Remember the pages with diagrams of different kinds of carburetors? They started near the middle of page 112. You know . . . in the big book."

"What *are* you talking about, Winsley?"

"Never mind the pages. The main thing is Gramps's plane has a problem," I answered, taking a swig of milk.

Dimples stopped eating. "What kind of problem?"

"Carburetor."

Dimples didn't answer.

"I think I can fix it," I continued.

"Really? Are you sure? I mean . . . not many people know about carburetors . . . and stuff like that."

"Well, I do. Remember the chapter about carburetors in one of our Bookmobile books?"

Dimples took a bite out of the middle of her sandwich. "No, I do not."

"I looked at those pages for so long, I must have memorized them, even the page numbers. Well, anyway, there's a screw that adjusts the amount of available gas. All it takes is small adjustments to allow a precise amount of fuel to pass the needle valve and . . ."

Dimples nodded but her eyes had a strange faraway look.

I knew Dimples wasn't getting any of what I was saying, so I finished my sentence as quickly as possible. "And anyway . . . I think I can fix it."

Expecting to hear something along the lines of

"You're one smart cookie," or something similar, I was stunned when Dimples pointed toward the elementary school and said, "I think you may have a bigger problem than a carburetor."

I looked just in time to see a flash of turquoise skidding out of the school's parking lot. For once, Dimples was wrong. I had two problems and they were racing down the road in Gramps's turquoise T-Bird. I should have known that crackpot grandfather of mine and that little-booger-of-a-brother would pull some kind of stunt while I was at school and the rest of family was away. Why else would they be flying home in the middle of the day?

I handed what was left of my sandwich to Dimples. "I gotta go home."

"Go. I'll throw your trash away and sign you out in the clinic book."

"Are you sure?" I asked, jumping down from the stone wall.

"Of course, I'm sure. Now, get going."

"Thanks, Dimples. About signing me out . . . there's a chance I'll get caught which means you could, too."

Dimples nodded. "So what? We'll worry about that later. Now, go on . . . while you've got the chance."

I smiled and turned away, making my walk seem slow and carefree, I sauntered toward the gate at the edge of the playground and hung around there for a couple of minutes until the teacher on duty wasn't looking. Then, I opened the gate and ran like my life depended on it.

I took every shortcut I knew in hopes of catching up with Gramps and Billy, but they were speeding home in a car and I was on foot.

By the time Gramps's house came into view, I had to stop running to catch my breath. Between gulps of air, a flash of green hopped around Gramps's house. At the sight of it, I broke into a trot but instead of darting around the house, I dove through Gramps's front door and dashed right back out, by way of Granny's kitchen.

As the screen door slammed shut behind me, I nearly collided with *Emerald Eyes*. Trundling along in the little seat behind Gramps sat Billy with a huge grin on his face. Thankfully, the third seat was empty.

Gramps, too, had a wide smile on his face and was wearing an old timey-looking leather helmet that came from heaven-knows-where.

I motioned for him to cut the engine. Of course, he didn't.

I ran along side and yelled with all of my might. "Gramps, what are you doing? Where are you going?"

"Trying to make it over to the other side of the train tracks – out to the meadow. Then we can pick up some speed and this here baby can take to the sky."

"I don't think taking off without any of the adults here is a good idea," I shouted back.

Gramps pulled the chin strap on his hat tighter and yelled, "Gotta try it out before I start hauling passengers. We'll be back soon enough."

"Cut the motor," I yelled as loud as I could, not knowing how much longer I could keep up with the small plane.

"No."

"Cut the motor, Gramps."

"No."

"CUT THE MOTOR . . . NOW!"

"Don't tell ME what to do. I'll do what I want, young lady," Gramps called.

Not knowing what else to do, I screamed, "Let me go, too."

"Well, now, you're talking," Gramps yelled as he yanked the helmet off of his head and turned off the motor.

Through a little round passenger window, Billy shook his fist at me. Through the green Dacron I heard, "Don't stop, Gramps. It's a trick. Didn't I tell you she'd ruin this for us? She's a pain in the neck. One big PAIN IN THE NECK!"

Gramps leaned out of the plane and said, "Now, you looky here, Winnie-girl. Your Granny phoned saying she was comin' home some time today and I need to get this plane in the air before havin' to deal with her. So, if you're going with us, give me your hand and I'll pull you on up. But if this is some kind of trick, then step aside and let us go. And I mean it."

"Gramps, I'm not trying to stop you but its gonna take a minute or two."

"Now see here, girl, is you is or is you isn't comin'?"

"Gramps, you have to believe me. I'm trying to help you . . . honestly, I am."

"Like you were when you called the police on me? Didn't think I knew about that, did you?"

"Okay, you're right. But that was THEN and this is NOW."

"So?"

I took a deep breath. "You've got to listen to me. Something's wrong but I can fix it. You've got to listen. I know what I'm taking about. Getting up more speed in the meadow isn't going to solve your problem. You may get *Emerald Eyes* up in the air or even speed her up a bit, but that's not going to keep her from sputtering and spurting and falling back down. If anything, it'll just be a further and harder fall when she does come back down."

"Nah . . . I think you're wrong. More than likely, the motor just needs to be broken in."

Gramps made a move as if to turn the ignition key back on.

I tried again, "Gramps, you've got to trust me on this. I wouldn't lie to you."

Billy tapped Gramps on his shoulder. "Yes, she would. She's nuts. Let's go."

I knew this was the moment. Either I had to keep *Emerald Eyes* on the ground for good or do all I could to make her safe. "Gramps, PLEASE. Give me five minutes with the motor and then, I'll go up with you. I promise. Pleeease."

"What?"

"You heard me. Come on, Gramps. Five minutes. That's all I'm asking."

"Well, okay. And Winnie-girl . . ."

"Yes?"

"I didn't figure you'd ever be one to take to the skies," Gramps said as he climbed down from the plane.

"Well then, you figured wrong," I called over my shoulder as I ran toward the garage for a screwdriver.

By the time I got back, my legs were trembling and my hands were shaking. It was one thing to make something safe for yourself to fly in, but another when you were making it safe for other people, too.

I dragged the ladder over from the side of the house and climbed up a few rungs to look down in the engine. It took a couple of minutes of searching until I found the carburetor and spark plugs. The pistons, two rods that went up and down depending on the air flow, were where they should be too. With the right amount of air, the spark plugs would create a spark, causing the pistons to go up and down, which in turn caused the gasoline to burn and the motor to run. The trick was to get in the exact amount of air needed to create the much-needed spark. I wasn't sure if I could do it . . . but I was going to give it my all. I blocked out everything and shut my eyes so that my mind would flip open the big engine book to page 112. I opened my eyes and twisted the screwdriver. I kept working as I skimmed both pages 113 and 114. As soon as I finished page 115, the words became blurry and I prayed I had it right. Either way, we'd soon find out – all of Cross Lanes, too.

Earlier, Gramps must have carried a piece of plywood to the train tracks because now it was ready for the wheels of *Emerald Eyes* to roll across in order to get to the other side.

I climbed down from the ladder and put it to the side while Gramps started the motor.

He and Billy rolled past Granny's rosebushes and headed for the tracks. I walked behind, feeling relieved the plane's motor sounded better and it was no longer hopping on the ground.

Emerald Eyes made a couple of groans as Gramps drove it across the plywood.

I waited to pull the plywood off of the tracks before using the plane's tire braces to hoist myself up and into the plane. I climbed into the seat with Billy. I could have sat behind him . . . but well . . . if things went wrong, I wanted to be within reach of him. I gave him a hug he didn't return and then put on the goggles Gramps threw over his shoulder toward me. My legs were all trembly like Granny's washing machine spinning a heavy load.

Gramps yelled over his shoulder, "We're off to the end of the rainbow and we're not coming back until we find that big ole pot of gold. Imagine that!"

Billy grabbed my hand as the plane's engine sputtered and whined.

I shut my eyes and prayed.

In no time at all, we were racing across the meadow.

Then, we lifted for a second and touched back down.

My stomach did a flip-flop and I squeezed Billy's hand back.

Another lift.

Another drop back down.

And then, we lifted . . . and lifted . . . and lifted . . . and didn't touch back down.

I opened my eyes, giggled and thanked God we were alive and we were FLYING!

The plane's engine roared as we flew over tops of cars.

We flew over rooftops.

We flew over treetops.

And then, we flew over the middle school. We were so close, we could have jumped out and walked across the roof. But of course, we stayed put.

Kids lining up after kickball looked up.

We looked down.

Their mouths were moving but we couldn't hear their words.

We waved.

They waved back.

The engine was loud. The smell of gasoline filled the air. And even now and then, *Emerald Eyes* gave a funny little shiver and shake but I didn't care as we circled all of Cross Lanes.

The people of Cross Lanes twisted and turned to watch us. If we'd had a horn, we would have honked it.

We flew around Cross Lanes Elementary about a million times. Finally, Hinkle came out. She shaded her eyes with her hands as she watched us. Then, she put her hands on her hips and stomped back inside. As she disappeared from sight, I knew I was living the most glorious moment of my life.

We flew here and we flew there.

We giggled, we laughed and we screamed.

And then, the three of us turned quiet as we watched a beat-up old station wagon make its way up the hillside and come to a stop in front of Gramps's house. Morse Withers. The door to the station wagon burst open and out stepped Granny. She cupped her hands to her moving mouth but we couldn't make out her words. Of course, we didn't need to hear to know what she was saying. She motioned with her arm for us to get down out of the sky. Gramps answered with a sharp turn toward Charleston and off we flew.

In no time at all, we were soaring above Charleston, our capital city. I felt a little nervous as I looked down at all of the concrete – sidewalks, unfamiliar buildings and streets. I would rather fall to earth among the trees and birds in Gramps's meadow than to be splattered on some street in Charleston. Billy must have been thinking the same thing because he grabbed my hand again and didn't let go.

And then . . . the shiny gold dome of the capitol building came into view, gleaming in the sunlight like a beckoning spotlight.

Gramps yelled, "There's our pot of gold!"

We flew toward the shiny dome and made a big loop around it. I wanted to reach out and swoop some of the gold up in my hand – or hang on to the pointy top, but of course, I couldn't. We were close, but not that close.

After another half loop, Gramps followed the Kanawha River and we headed toward home, veering off only to circle the little brick house Mother was hoping to buy. I don't know how Gramps knew it was the one. Of course, Gramps seemed to know everything.

Throughout our flight, I kept checking the little floating ping-pong ball Gramps had rigged up in a clear plastic cylinder. It was our gas gauge and as long as the ball stayed afloat, we'd be safe.

A couple of clouds later, we were back in Cross Lanes. I strained to see if Granny was still outside.

She was. Her suitcase was beside her and Morse Withers was still standing there, too. It appeared neither of them had moved since we flew off, but I knew Granny had, because she'd pulled the flag she and Gramps flew on national holidays from its holder on the porch rail. Now, she was waving it back-and-forth like a starter at the Indy 500.

As I peered down at Granny, I noticed something else. Something bad. Really bad. Something sure to kill all of us. That is, if we chanced to live when Gramps attempted to land *Emerald Eyes*.

Gramps must have noticed, too, because he was pointing to Mother and Daddy who were sprinting toward Granny, Morse and the flag.

Billy screamed, "What the heck are they doing home?"

Gramps didn't answer, so I yelled back, "This can't be good."

"Good?" Billy answered as he pulled off his goggles. "Are you kidding? Good? We're the ones as GOOD as dead."

"Well, it's not my fault," I replied, letting go of his hand.

Billy yanked his goggles off. "They can get mad all they want but I've got to go to the bathroom first. And yes, Winsely, it is YOUR fault. You're the one who fixed the plane so it would fly, or have you forgotten that?"

"No, I haven't forgotten." Maybe I should have felt worried, but deep-down, I felt proud. It had been me – a sixth-grade girl, and one who wasn't even the best student at the middle school, for that matter.

As Gramps eased the plane toward the ground, I was tempted to shut my eyes but I didn't. It'd be like cheating. A person brave enough to fly in a homemade plane should be able to keep their eyes open when it landed. So, I did.

The ground came up.

We went down.

It was as simple as that. Scary, but simple.

A couple of high bounces and we were rolling through daisies and dandelions toward the train track.

Gramps shoved the plane's gear to neutral and we all sat frozen until Billy yelled, "Yahooooo!"

I hopped out and ran to get the plywood to put back on the tracks.

Once everything was ready, I gave Gramps the thumbs-up.

He shoved the gear forward and the engine gave the sound of thousand humming bees as *Emerald Eyes* started across the plywood.

The plane was close to reaching the other side when its back tire slipped off of the plywood and landed between two railroad ties.

Gramps cussed and climbed over the side of the plane. After dropping to the ground, his face turned red as he tugged at the wheel. "These railroad ties are too close. Tire's lodged. Can't be moved. Gonna need some strong men to help me lift that dang wheel out of there."

"Are you sure, Gramps?" I asked.

"Yeah, I'm sure. It's lodged in place."

"Drats."

"Yeah, you can say that again," he answered.

Then my heart sank.

THE DISTANT WHISTLE OF THE 3:45!

Disaster was chugging down the tracks and coming our way.

Gramps gave another tug on the tire and managed to lift it slightly for a second or two. Immediately, the plane dropped back down, causing Gramps to smack his head on the underside of the wing's metal frame. At exactly the same time, Billy's foot came through the floorboard.

A LOUDER WHISTLE FROM THE 3:45!

I waited for Gramps to scramble back into the plane for Billy but he only rocked back-and-forth holding his head singing, "The wee little leprechauns are our friends."

I wanted to bolt but there was no one else to save Billy . . . or Gramps. I knew without looking that Daddy, Mother, Morse and Granny were still too far away to reach us in time.

THE DESPERATE WHISTLE FROM THE 3:45!

Gramps continued singing. "Leprechauns eat gold for breakfast and four-leaf clovers for their snack" was getting louder, too. Even so, he didn't drown out the sound of the train.

I prayed for some feisty little leprechaun to appear with his shillelagh stick to whack Gramps over the head, but nothing happened. No leprechaun, no shillelagh stick, only Gramps with a knot on his head, singing at the top of his lungs, dancing an Irish jig.

In the midst of all of the singing and whistle-blowing, I'd forgotten about Billy until he yelled, "Someooooone sssaaavvveee meeeee!"

Hoping to sound more confident than I felt, I answered, "You'll be alright. Don't panic."

I shaded my eyes with my hand and peered down the tracks. And there it was, the extremely small, but distant, outline of an engine.

Trying not to panic, I turned back to Billy and yelled, "Billy, try to work your foot loose."

"Can't!"

"Try to wiggle your foot." I yelled again.

Gramps had one leg over the side of the plane as if to climb back in. Quickly, I grabbed a belt loop on the back of his pants. "Come with me, Gramps, if you want to kiss the Blarney stone."

He put his leg back on the ground and staggered like he was going to faint.

With both hands, I got a firm grip on both belt loops and pulled him away from the plane. and slung him under a nearby weeping willow tree.

THE *COVER-YOUR-EARS-AND-RUN-FOR-THE-HILLS* WHISTLE OF THE 3:45 . . . LOUDER, MUCH LOUDER!!!

Worse, I felt small vibrations beneath my feet from the approaching train.

I ran to *Emerald Eyes* and ducked my head under her small belly.

Billy was wailing at the top of his lungs.

I pushed up on the bottom of his shoe with every little bit of strength I could muster.

Nothing.

I made a fist and pounded Billy's heel back through the broken boards.

Even though his shoe shot through the bits of shattered wood, there it stayed.

I watched to make sure his foot wasn't going to come back down before crawling out from under the plane, all the while screaming, "Jump, Billy. NOW!"

I willed myself not to even glance down the train track. Instead, I looked up at Billy. To my horror, he was frozen in midair. His finger pointed toward the track. I didn't need to see what he saw. I knew from the hard pounding of stronger vibrations, disaster was not slowing down.

THE *EAR-SPLITTING AWFUL* WHISTLE OF THE 3:45 FILLED THE AIR WITH AN EQUALLY HORRENDOUS SCREECH!

I turned to look for Dad but he was still only a black silhouette far away and couldn't reach us in time.

Saving Billy was up to me.

I clawed my way up to Billy and pulled him over the edge of the plane. I gave him a hard push and jumped down behind him. Without a second to spare, we both ran for safety as soon as our feet hit the ground.

THE *BLAST-YOU-TO-KINGDOM-COME, LOUDER THAN I THOUGHT POSSIBLE,* WHISTLE OF THE 3:45 SHATTERED THE AIR!

Under the thin branches of the willow tree, the three of us fell to our knees, ducked our heads and covered our ears as bolts, nails, boards, tires and wires flew through the air.

It was a tornado of racket, a tornado of fear, a tornado of destruction that pierced the air for a hundred years.

The screech of metal bounced around my body and through my head.

Eventually, the indescribable ringing in my ears ended when the 3:45 came to a grinding halt, I knew without looking, *Emerald Eyes* was no more.

After two attempts to stand on legs that buckled under me, I was finally able to get up and stay up. And when I did, I was right. *Emerald Eyes* was strung out in the meadow in a million little pieces. Parts were smoldering and here and there and small bits of green Dacron were burning as they flapped from the branches of scraggly apple trees dotting the landscape. The smell of gasoline and burning rubber filled the air. Even though I was standing in the middle of a war zone, I knew the real war hadn't started yet.

Daddy and Morse were the first to reach us.

Mother and Granny were close behind.

Daddy said, "Holy Moly, are the three of you alright?"

Mother sobbed as she ran her hands over my entire body from head-to-toe, as if checking for something missing, broken or in the wrong place. After doing the same to Billy, she blubbered, "I knew this was going to happen. I knew it."

Granny's hand went to her heart. I hoped she wasn't going to faint or die ... or anything but couldn't blame her if she did. I felt like I was going to topple over, myself. But after a couple of good looks around, Granny clucked her tongue, folded her arms and stomped her foot.

Billy had wet his pants and limped to stand behind me, which let me know that his ankle was probably sprained.

The engineer of the 3:45 came running up. "You folk all alive?"

Gramps flipped a small willow branch from his shoulder. "Guess we'll be hoofin' it in the future."

I patted his arm, knowing he'd gotten his mind back and he'd be lucky if Mother and Granny let him live.

As I pulled splinters from my hair, I heard a siren. *Drats.*

It went without saying, Chief Knight and all of Cross Lanes was going to be talking about this for years to come.

Across the meadow, a crowd of bobbing heads made their way toward us. I bent down and whispered in Billy's ear, "Get going or you're gonna get caught in your wet pants."

Billy hobbled off as I brushed another twig from my shoulder.

If this was the pot at the end of the rainbow, no wonder leprechauns tucked four-leaf clovers in their hatbands and disappeared from sight.

Chapter 18

~ Mother's Meltdown ~

~ Worry #19 ~

Mother is going to kill

All of us –

If Granny, Chief Knight or Dad

Doesn't beat us to a pulp first.

After Chief Knight made a big show of putting out a few teeny-tiny fires that would have probably gone out on their own, he turned toward us and said, "I'll be back later to discuss all of this. There are ramifications, you know. People can't expect to cause this kind of commotion and then just go on as if nothing happened. Yes, indeed, there are ramifications. Someone's gonna pay."

Mother grabbed my shoulder and yanked me all the way home. Dad followed, making small whistling noises. Granny peeled away from the group and stomped toward her own house. Gramps trotted behind her, saying, "C'mon, you gotta know the real reason I picked *Emerald Eyes* in the first place is because the color reminded me of your own gorgeous hazely-green eyes, sweetie pie."

Granny replied, "My eyes are blue, you old fool."

She kept marching and even though Gramps's legs were longer, he had to take two quick steps to keep up with one of hers. If he *was* scared, it didn't keep him from throwing a wave our way.

Mother forbid us to wave back to the "almost killer of her own two kids."

Before we reached our house, I glanced toward Gramps just as he was about to enter his own house. He might have lost his beloved emerald-eyed baby, but I guess the fact he'd shown off in front of Cross Lanes was really what counted. Even from the distance, I could see he was wearing a huge grin on his face.

I nodded and tried not to smile, knowing it wouldn't do for Mother to see anything close to a grin on my own face.

As soon as we entered the kitchen, Mother reached for the bottle of *Dempsy's Diarrhea Concoction* she'd started keeping by the bread box. She twirled the cap off so quickly, it flew through the air. She took a long swig of golden-brown liquid, and whirled around yelling, "WHAT WERE YOU THINKING? What WERE you thinking? What in the name of 'tarnation WERE you thinking?"

Her face was as red as Chief Knight's fire truck. Her whole body was shaking from head to toe.

Dad pulled out a chair from the table and reached for her arm as he led her to it.

The phone rang. Dad took it off the hook and let it dangle toward the floor.

Mother dropped her head on the table and sobbed – loud, long sobs with little screams sprinkled in.

Dad turned on the faucet and ran a dish towel under the water. He walked over to Mother and placed it across her forehead. She never looked up and the sobbing didn't stop.

The longer Mother cried, the more scared I felt.

Billy was still wearing his old clothes and every so often, I got a whiff of his earlier accident. Dad must have, too, because he said, "Billy, go change your pants and then, git back in here."

Billy muttered, "Yes, sir."

Since I hadn't heard him say "sir" in a hundred years, I knew he was scared, too.

He left and came back wearing a different pair of pants.

Mother continued to cry.

Dad looked at us and pointed toward the kitchen table.

Billy sat down.

I sat down.

Dad sat down.

Still, Mother continued to cry.

And there the four of us sat for another hundred years until Mother's crying-jag seemed to come to an end.

She blew her nose on the corner of the tablecloth, raised her head, took a look at us and started in again.

Drats.

At that point I wanted to get it over and done with – punishment and all. I took a deep breath, tapped her shoulder and said, "It was my fault."

"You?" Mother said. "You didn't order the plans. You didn't build the plane. You didn't fly the plane."

"But . . . I . . . I . . . uh . . ." I stammered.

Mother didn't answer me. Instead, she turned to Dad and said, "Will, that crazy dad of yours is the reason both of our children came close to meeting their Maker today!"

Dad got up from the table and took himself a

swig of *Dempsy's* before muttering, "Maybe we should concentrate on the fact that they didn't."

Mother let out another sob and screamed, "NO, THEY DIDN'T . . . but if they had crossed over, it would have been HIS FAULT!"

Feeling as if I was going to explode, I jumped up. "DON'T blame Gramps. It was MY fault."

Mother wasn't one to listen to things about books, carburetors and Hinkle but she'd have to listen now.

As I cleared my throat to tell it all, Billy jumped in, "Blame Winsley. It WAS her fault. She fixed the plane."

I nodded in agreement. "Billy's right. I'm the one who read the books and I'm the one who knew how to adjust the carburetor, so yes, blame me – not Gramps."

Mother's jaw dropped and for just a second, I thought I saw Daddy grin.

Neither said a word as I began to talk.

And talk.

And talk some more.

I threw in everything I knew about lift and thrust . . . and carburetors . . . and pistons . . . and angles of attack. I said it all. Half-hoping to distract them and half-hoping to impress them. After all, I was the reason, maybe the only reason, we'd shown all of Cross Lanes, people in Charleston, too. Maybe that was what everyone should be talking about, and not the fact that we are a family of crackpots who do things differently, things that no one else dares to do.

Every now and again, Billy would add something I'd forgotten or left out.

Throughout it all, even though Daddy smiled a time or two, Mother's stern expression never changed, nor did she say a word. Not even when I finished talking.

When I ran out of breath and couldn't think of another word to say, there was silence for a minute or two until Daddy said "Git yourselves to bed, now."

Safe in my room, I thought it only fair to finish documenting what I started. Normally, I had pencils all over the place but the only one I could find was good old Leprechaun Green – of course.

WE FlEW!

WaHoo! WAHOO! WAHOOOOO!

Nothing more was said about our escapade until a day later when Mother fought back with a rope from the hardware. She tied it to the end of Granny's clothesline, looped a couple trees and anchored it to a stake. The whole thing made a long line between our house and Gramps and Granny's.

She didn't say a word. She didn't have to. We knew if we crossed over that rope, she'd kill us and maybe Gramps, too.

Luckily, Mother never noticed every time either Billy or I left the house to go to Grayson's or anywhere, Gramps's turquoise car left his house, too.

Even though, Chief Knight never showed up to talk about any "ramifications," the rope stayed up.

Gradually, Granny began riding around with us in Gramps's car and enjoyed slurping milkshakes and ice cream cones at the Dairy Queen, where every now and then, we signed an autograph or two.

Chapter 19

~ Moving to Siberia ~

~ WORRY #WHATEVER ~

WE'RE leaving Cross Lanes,

THE center of the Universe!

Okay, so it's not Siberia,

Only thirty minutes down the road.

It's NOT Cross Lanes,

So it might as well be Siberia!

Okay, so I lost count of my worries. That's a good thing. I haven't kept up my worry-numbers because lately because I've been worrying a whole lot less.

After all, I've been in a plane crash – kinda, and I'm alive to tell about it.

I've been in a train wreck – kinda, and again, I'm alive to tell about it.

Better yet, I've soared through the sky and most importantly, all over Cross Lanes . . . and I proved old bat Hinkle wrong. Considering everything, I hardly ever worry about anything now because it feels so good to be alive.

The fact is I didn't worry for awhile until I overheard one of Mother's phone conversations. It went something like this:

"I tell you, it's the last straw. Personally, I think a change will do us good," Mother said into the phone's mouthpiece.

I wanted to inch closer in hopes of identifying the voice on the other end, but Mother had fire in her eyes and I was afraid to make any sudden moves.

I slipped out of the kitchen and darted to the den. With the precision of a surgeon, I picked up the receiver there and listened.

After a brief period of silence, I heard Mother's voice again. "I was wondering if you could show us that cute little brick house just off the main road on the way to Charleston?"

"I'd love to. If you're free around five today, we could meet there then," A familiar voice answered. I couldn't match a face to the voice but it was definitely a voice I knew.

Mother cleared her throat. "Today is fine."

"Then, today it is, although I must say that I'm surprised that you would call ME after all, well, you know . . . the notes and all."

Oh, my gosh. Mother was making good on her threat. And OLD BAT HINKLE was going to guide the way. What could possibly be worse? To that, Mother might answer "two dead kids and an old man sprawled across the train tracks."

Mother cleared her throat for a second time. "Actually, I was surprised not to get more notes about Billy's behavior from you than I did."

"Really?"

"Really. In fact, it was one of his best years."

"You don't say." Hinkle answered with a laugh.

"Well, I need to get a move on if we're going to meet at five," Mother replied.

"See you then."

I put the receiver down and tried to consider how much better moving to the little brick house would be on Mother. Daddy, too. But what about Billy? He'd be devastated. And what about Gramps? Would he survive losing us now that he'd lost *Emerald-Eyes*? Who would live in our house? How would my friends find me? How often would I get back to visit? What about school? Did the kids in the red brick house – if there ever were any kids, go to my school? Where would I go to school? And Granny? Taking us away from Gramps was taking us away from Granny, too. And that just wouldn't do.

Someone had to bring Mother to her senses and I guess that someone had to be me. I found her in the bathroom powdering her face.

"Mother, are you sure . . . really sure, moving is the right thing to do?"

"Were you listening in my conversation, young lady?"

"Yes, yes I was. But Mother, this is the only life we've ever known. We can't move."

Mother stood up and reached for her purse. "Why don't you get ready and come with me? That way, you can see for yourself. You're gonna love it there. We all are."

I put on my sneakers and in no time flat, we were slamming car doors and walking toward the old bat at the little brick house. I wanted to flee as she smiled and motioned for us to enter.

The little brick house was just that – little and brick. But for some strange reason, Mother oohed and aaahed over everything from faucets to hinges. To me, it looked rather ordinary, but Mother acted like it was the most wonderful house on the face of the earth. And maybe it was – to her. After all, it was more than spitting distance from Gramps.

We took the grand tour – which took all of two

minutes before Mother asked if we could see the house right across the street that was up for sale also.

Hinkle looked down at me with a smirk before answering. "That house, my dears, is already promised to another family."

"Really? Oh, I do hope we get good neighbors," Mother replied.

"I do believe they'll be the perfect neighbors . . . certainly, ones you deserve."

I wanted to remind Hinkle we hadn't bought anything yet, but I kept still.

Hinkle continued, "Yes, I'd want you to have neighbors like family."

Mother smiled as if Hinkle was giving us a compliment of some kind. I wasn't so sure. If anything, I'd bet we were looking at the sort of neighbors that gun their motorcycles in the dead of night and do their bow-and-arrow target practice our way. A mangy cat and a couple of snarly dogs were a given. Maybe a smelly pig, too.

No matter what I thought, it was evident the wheels were in motion. It seemed Mother was determined to keep things rolling along at a brisk pace. It became evident her weapon of choice to fight Gramps was to roll us down the road and into the little brick house. As if to make her case, she was constantly talking about "the unfortunate incident" and "not wantin' to bury kids" in the same breath.

People in Cross Lanes were talking, too. I'd heard things like "Any man fool enough to stop a train ought to be sent away – far away" or "It's a wonder half of Cross Lanes is alive today."

In the end, a sold sign went up in the yard of the little brick house and another one in the yard across the street from it. We didn't know who bought the second one because Hinkle stopped answering her phone.

The night before we left Cross Lanes, I couldn't sleep and slipped out of my bed to look out my window. I pulled my old lace curtains to the side and then hid behind them when I spotted a shadowy figure taking down Mother's rope in the moonlight.

I thought about waking Daddy but figured since we were moving, what harm could there be in letting go of the rope. Instead, I watched Gramps sling it on his shoulder and disappear in the darkness.

The next morning when we said our last goodbyes, I gave both Gramps and Granny an extra tight hug and my brightest smile.

I'd dreaded this moment for weeks, expecting weeping and wailing, and maybe even some flailing around on the floor, but Gramps and Granny seemed fine. In fact, if anything they acted like they were in a hurry for us to go. For old people, if they were putting on an act, they were doing a humdinger of good job.

In fact, it was Mother, Dad, Billy and me wiping our eyes and sobbing ourselves silly.

We stayed that way until we arrived at the little brick house and Hinkle came by to let us know that our new neighbors would be moving in across the street in a day or two. She'd always acted strange. But if anything, she'd gotten worse. Between every other word, a giggle escaped her. Strange behavior, I thought – especially for someone like Hinkle.

Later, I mentioned Hinkle's odd behavior to Mother. "Don't you think Miss Hinkle acted kinda silly?"

"Oh, I don't know. Edith has always been a little different. Maybe she's just excited about making two commissions, one on the sale of this house and one on the house across the street."

I nodded and Mother continued, "I declare, I don't know who in their right mind would buy on the other side of the street. I do believe you could build a boat and float right on out to the Gulf of Mexico in that creek behind it."

"What?" I answered, with a small twitch, the first one in weeks.

Mother didn't bother to answer as she walked down the hall toward the kitchen.

I tried to dismiss thoughts of boat building, but my twitch shot off again and a couple butterflies came back home.

Apparently, Billy had been listening to our conversation because he poked his head out of his bedroom and looked at me with his eyes opened wide – owl wide.

I shot back a "don't even think about it" look with a couple a twitches thrown in for free.

He disappeared into his room and I prayed it really was the thought of two fat commissions that had Hinkle acting a fool.

Luckily, there wasn't any time to worry. We were too busy doing all the things you do when you move.

Every time Dad drove up with another load in the back of a pick-up truck he'd managed to borrow from a friend, we unloaded whatever he was hauling. Then we tugged, pushed and pulled whatever it was, inside the house. Afterwards, we kicked it and elbowed it in whatever direction Mother pointed.

Mentally, I was planning a sleep-over with my now old friends – the ones back Cross Lanes and wondering exactly how much closer we lived to the library in Charleston. I imagined the fun of telling my new yet-to-be friends that I helped build an airplane, flew all over the place in it, and lived to tell about it! I mean, who wouldn't want to be friends with a kid like me.

Later that evening as Daddy bolted my totem pole to frame of my bed, I said, "Dad, I'm beginning to see what you mean about the other *ninety-eight*."

"What other *ninety-eight?*"

"The other *ninety-eight PERCENT*. You know, the *ninety-eight percent* of things that never come to be."

"Well . . . little girl, I hate to tell you this, but I made that up."

"What?"

"I thought you needed to hear it at the time."

I burst out laughing and so did he.

I thought for a moment about how really lucky we were to have survived the whole plane-thing. "Dad, I think I've learned something."

"What's that, little one?" he replied, with a laugh.

"Well, it doesn't seem like worrying about something will change it, so it's kinda a waste to worry in the first place."

"Good for you. Takes most people a lifetime to figure that one out."

"And Dad . . . I was wondering why you and Mother came back early from Canton? Was it because you were missing us?"

"Why do you think we came back?" Dad asked.

"Well, I'd like to think that you were missing us or that Mother and you had a feeling that something was wrong – you know, sixth sense kind-of-thing or something."

"I hate to tell you this but we came back because the Football Hall of Fame was holding a ceremony and we didn't take clothes dressy enough to attend."

We both laughed. Me, especially.

"Think you'll ever go back?" I asked.

"Go back?"

"To Canton."

"Maybe, but not until you and Billy are full-grown, with kids of your own and your mom thinks it's safe to leave you," he answered with another hearty laugh.

"Dad, I love that my bedroom is on the front of the house but I'm not wild about yellow. Any chance we can scrape up money to paint it a different color?"

"I don't think see why not, although I doubt that your mother would go for any shade of green, especially if its anywhere near the hue of emerald."

We both laughed.

"What about pale lavender?" I asked.

"Lavender, it is," he answered. "And by the way, I noticed you've been calling me "Dad" instead of "Daddy" lately. I like it. Makes you sound older. Just don't go getting too old to give your dad a hug every now and then. Okay?"

"It's a deal," I answered with a hug.

As we stood back and looked at my bedposts, we burst out laughing.

Both Mother and Billy came in my room and wanted to know what all the laughter was about. Soon, the two of them were laughing along with Dad and me. After my mattress was plopped across the box springs, the four of us jumped on top and lay there for the longest time, laughing at everything and nothing in particular.

I couldn't help but think we were off to a great beginning. Maybe moving was going to work out after all.

After a dinner of sandwiches and chips, I retreated to my new room to empty boxes. Afterwards, I joined Nancy Drew on her latest adventure until the stars came out. As I finished the last chapter and closed my book, I heard a car creep down the gravely road and into the driveway of the vacant house across the street.

When the motor cut off, the sound of two car doors brought me to my feet. I darted to my window.

I watched as shadowy figures disappeared through the front door. Then, someone blinked the porch light as the door shut behind them. And for just a second, a flash of light danced across a glimmer of turquoise and chrome. In that second, I vaguely wondered if the library had any books on how to how build the World's Smallest Cruise Ships and a giggle that started in my toes and ended with a smile across my face.

Billy tiptoed into my room and whispered, "Is it them?"

"You bet."

"I knew it would be," he answered as the lights went on across the street and two faces appeared in the window.

"Me, too."

As they waved, I flipped on the overhead light in my bedroom so they could see the two of us as we waved back.

And there we stayed, under the stars, waving our hands off for the longest time.

Chapter 20

~ Fifteen Years Later ~

These days Daddy spends his days walking in the yard swinging a golf club, as if he's ready for a round or two. He likes to tinker in his workshop and can fix just about anything.

Mother is the new bra-fitter in the "unmentionables" department at Stone & Thomas in Charleston. Unlike the days of the Red Bra Incident, today nothing is hung outside to dry. It all swirls-by in the dryer – safe from prying eyes.

Miss Dee LaPierre married Henry Strap, the owner of *Great Crepes and More*, Charleston's only French restaurant. I heard Mrs. Dee Strap (her new name) had planned on continuing as the math teacher at the middle school while Henry ran the restaurant. That is, until kids at Cross Lanes Elementary gave their little son Jacques a nickname. After that little "Jock Strap" was home-schooled.

You can find Edith Hinkle atop the paper's gossip column. On a daily basis, *Edith's Ear* keeps everyone abreast of West Virginia's "movers and shakers." More people seem to be working than *moving and shaking* so Hinkle's column is usually rather short. That is, until Granny sold the farm. For some strange reason, Hinkle droned on about it in the paper as if Granny had let go of Buckingham Palace. That same day Granny canceled her subscription, saying she didn't intend to be *moving and shaking* on page eight in front of strangers having their morning coffee.

Dimples Cheeksly got married and moved to Ohio. She and her husband have three little girls. As expected, all three have the cutest dimpley smiles. A few years back, Dimples and her husband opened the *Stone Wall Cafeteria* and now, neither she nor I have time to reminisce about the old days and have to make do with a quick phone call every now and then.

A couple of years ago, Granny took to painting small canvases of everyone who got sick in Cross Lanes. That way, if the person up and died, she had a souvenir (for lack of a better word) for their loved ones. In no time at all, phone calls from disgruntled friends and neighbors started coming in all hours of the day and night because if you sneezed or had the snuffles anywhere within her hearing, Granny was setting up her easel and reaching for her paint.

Fortunately, she's gone back to hauling flowers to the cemetery, always saving the most glorious bouquet for a certain someone.

Below is the newspaper clipping that never fails to make me smile. It's been taped above Granny's kitchen sink for the last several years.

> **Seth Walker** 77, of Cross Lanes, West Virginia passed away Monday afternoon in Charleston Memorial after a short bout of pneumonia. He will be sadly missed by Birdie, the love of his life, his only son Will, daughter-in-law Emmie, granddaughter Winsley and grandson Billy. A memorial service will be held Thursday at 2:00 at the Methodist church. Burial to follow at *Our Eternal Life*. Seth was an inventor who will be long remembered for looping the capitol in his tiny homemade plane. His last invention, *Music Inside Your Casket,* is still in use out at *Our Eternal Life*. On a windy day, if you stomp your foot beside one of the small windmills poking above some dearly departed's grave, you can often hear the faint sounds of *Oh, When the Saints Go Marching In* coming from the ground.

Most everybody thought Billy would end up in the pokey, but he proved us all wrong and even finished high school. Boy, did we all celebrate. Then, as if to pay us back for Granny's devotion to the dead, Mother's church work, and the prayers of the entire community, he decided to go into the ministry. Personally, I wasn't all that surprised. He was never the same after *that* day, the one where he looked the 3:45 dead in the eye.

There's hardly a day that I don't think of Gramps and the exhilaration I felt as Billy and I flew with him. It was a fabulous sensation, the memory of which never fails to make me smile.

At the beginning of this school year, as I was handing out math books to one of my new students, he asked me, "Are you the real Winsley Walker, the one who circled the Capitol in a homemade plane?" It was then that I knew Gramps's legacy to me was more than his old set of McGuffey readers. His legacy was my *can-do* attitude, the one that makes me confident and less prone to worry nowadays. In the past, I worried about some downright silly things . . . some serious things, too. But the worrying didn't change anything. What was going to happen was going to happen, no matter what I thought.

Shoot . . . maybe all that happened was Gramps's way of getting me ready to face real life.

And I have . . . twenty-some students at a time.

~ About tHE AutHOR ~

Nancy Cadle, the real Winsley Walker, grew up in Cross Lanes, West Virginia. She and her younger brother Tim, along with her parents John and Thelma Cadle lived next door to her father's parents Orval and Dessie Cadle.

Situations in this novel are greatly embellished, although many are grounded in fact. Nancy's grandfather did show up every evening in the family's backyard, usually with a croquet mallet, baseball or kite in his hand.

Weekends were often spent at her grandfather's farm where Nancy and her brother were sent on errands atop a John Deere tractor and a car's headlights did round the curve as her grandfather was dancing his way to "Little Egypt" in the middle of the night.

Nancy's grandfather did surprise them all with

a shiny new T-bird, but it was a buttery beige, not turquoise, and although her grandfather enjoyed tinkering on this-n-that, he didn't build an airplane.

However, the legacy he left was exactly like Seth Walker's in this story: if you were born a Cadle, you were capable of conquering the world. So they did, each in their own way

Much like his grandfather, Tim Cadle, the real Billy Walker, loves to tinker with this-n-that and is the go-to person when something mechanical needs to be repaired. He lives his life surrounded by the love of his wife Carla, five grown children, and seven grandchildren. Today, he still loves being atop a John Deere, even if it's only a riding mower. He ends each day outside and more often than not, friends and family gather at his house to eat, talk, and laugh.

Nancy and Tim's mother, Thelma Cadle, spent much of her life in church like Emmie Walker. Thelma served on various committees for Cross Lanes Methodist and could usually be found in the church kitchen cleaning up after a pot luck supper or picnic. Later, she and her husband John were members of the same Sunday school class for over 40 years at Broadmoor United Methodist, in Baton Rouge, Louisiana.

On more than one occasion, Thelma sent her husband John Cadle, the real Will Walker, next door to talk to his dad about not under-minding her authority with "Billy." Once there, the conversation was usually much like the one in this book.

There really was a little brick house for sale on the way to Charleston, but when the family moved from West Virginia to Louisiana it was for a better job opportunity for John.

As for Nancy, she and Ron Craddock were married in the sanctuary at Cross Lanes Methodist surrounded by their friends and family. Soon after, they made their way to Baton Rouge, Louisiana where both graduated from Louisiana State University. Ten years later, while living in Houston, Texas, their son Josh was born. Now, Nancy and Ron live on Lake Lanier, outside of Atlanta, Georgia, where they enjoy spending time with Josh and his family who live nearby.

After teaching elementary students for over three decades, Nancy still reaches for a book or her electronic reader when granddaughter Kaitlyn comes to visit. As they enter an imaginary time and place, Nancy often says a silent prayer of thanks for all of the good that's come her way and often glances at the mantel where a set of well-worn McGuffey readers stand watch across the room.

~ Acknowledgments ~

This work-of-the-heart could not have been completed without the following people:

Ron Craddock – who always believed in my ability to put on paper the embellished and exaggerated emotions, humor and events of my childhood.

WINGS (Writers in North Georgia) – without their faith in me I would have lost all hope of making my desire a reality. Thank you to Connie Fleming, Maureen McDaniel, Mary Ann Rodman, Stephanie Swerdloff Fenton Hickey, Susan Spain and T.K. Read. You are angels on earth.

Cross Lanes, West Virginia – the perfect place to learn the value of friendship and the love of family.